Reach the
  Right People,
Build Your
  Career Network,
and Land Your
  Dream Job—Now!

SUPERNETWORKING

MICHAEL SALMON

CAREER
PRESS
FRANKLIN LAKES, NJ

SuperNetworking
Edited by Nicole DeFelice
Typeset by Eileen Dow Munson
Cover design by Cheryl Cohan Finbow
Printed in the U.S.A. by Book-mart Press

To order this title, please call toll-free 1-800-CAREER-1 (NJ and Canada: 201-848-0310) to order using VISA or MasterCard, or for further information on books from Career Press.

**The Career Press, Inc., 3 Tice Road, PO Box 687,
Franklin Lakes, NJ 07417**
www.careerpress.com

Library of Congress Cataloging-in-Publication Data

Salmon, Michael, 1956-
    SuperNetworking : reach the right people, build your career network, and land your dream job—now! / by Michael Salmon.
        p. cm.
    Includes index.
    ISBN 1-56414-700-2 (pbk.)
    1. Business networks. 2. Social networks. 3. Career development.
    I. Title: SuperNetworking. II. Title.

HD69.S8S25 2004
650.1'3—dc21   2003054653

➤ Dedication

To Holly, Alex, Adrie, and Evan: Words can't describe what all of you mean to me.

To the readers: I worked for many years with job seekers and know what you are going through. I wrote this book as if I were standing next to you offering immediate, practical solutions. The intent was to share this methodology with as many people as possible, make a difference, and enhance your lives personally and professionally.

➤ Acknowledgments

Jacqueline Barbour who said to me, "You have enough material to write a book." Thank you for giving me the push to take this idea and turn it into a program that has helped thousands of people.

Carl Baskind, thank you for being my compass. Your patience, friendship, insight, candor, and support are greatly appreciated.

Gerry Sindell, thank you for believing in my concept. Your guidance, wisdom, enthusiasm, and friendship were inspirational.

Michael Snell, thank you for being an excellent teacher and raising the bar. You held me to a standard that resulted in the publication of my first book.

My wife, Holly, thank you for being the champion of my idea. Your undying support and belief provided the fuel for my engine. I love you.

My children Alexandra, Adrienne, and Evan, thank you for your words of encouragement and support. I hope this experience inspires all of you to reach for the stars.

To my parents, Otto and Anne, thank you for putting me on this Earth which has allowed me to share this program with countless others. Can you believe your son is an author?

Table of Contents

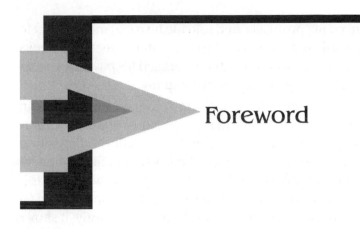

Foreword

I never saw myself as an author. Years ago, I was in the executive search business, placing senior level IT and financial services executives. One day I received a call from a man I didn't know I'll call him Joe. Joe mentioned that he had been given my name by a mutual friend, and he asked if I could give him a few minutes of my time. Joe said he had recently been laid off from his job-he had been a sales representative in ladies' lingerie for the same company for 19 years. As Joe talked, I heard a man who sounded hurt, scared, and confused. Although I didn't think that I could help him (because he was a friend of a friend), I invited him to come to my office and said that I might be able to give him some helpful tips on how to find his new job.

We spent a few hours going through the entire *SuperNetworking* plan, which at that time was more of an outline than a completed program. Joe took some notes, thanked me, and left. I didn't hear from him for six weeks. Then, out of the blue, I received a call from him. He sounded like a changed man.

He thanked me profusely, and told me he owed me his life. He had followed my program to the letter, and in just a few weeks had secured a great new job that leveraged his past sales experience with a fast-growing retail company.

I realized then what a difference *SuperNetworking* can make, and I decided then that I needed to share it with as many people as possible. Since then, I've dedicated myself to spreading the gospel about *SuperNetworking* to find your next job opportunity. And over the years, the people who have followed this plan have discovered that it is far more than just a way to get the job of your dreams. More importantly, it shows you how to create an invaluable network of relationships for life.

Job seekers need to know how to access and operate the entire job market, including areas where the hidden majority of available jobs are found. They also need to know how to maintain their network as their golden parachute forever. *SuperNetworking* is the only book that can teach you not only how to survive in, but how to thrive in a job market that is more competitive than ever before. Here, I have tried to show you that, now and for the foreseeable future, it will be our *networks* that will provide the continuity and security that long-term employment once provided to earlier generations.

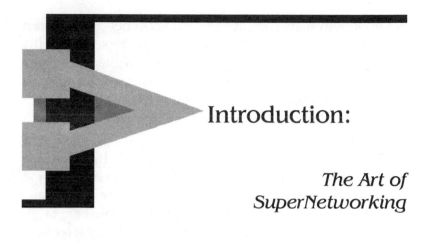

Introduction:

The Art of SuperNetworking

Is This You Now?

For most people, the process of finding a new job is up there on the pleasure scale with exploratory surgery—only to be undertaken when you have no choice. Whether you are actively seeking a new job, reentering the job market, making a career change, contemplating a job change but not actively looking, unhappily employed, or you expect to be downsized soon, you find yourself asking the question, *What's next in my career?* Because of the pressure to do something quick to find a job, many of you are not thinking clearly, even though you think you are. Some of you are not sleeping well; for others, even the best food doesn't taste all that great and nothing anyone says is really that funny. Could this be you that I'm describing?

You try to tell yourself to snap out of this funk. You know the job market is tight and saturated with highly qualified candidates who are finding that "great" jobs are few and far between. The truth is, the biggest problem is not that there are no jobs available, but it's the way most people approach the job market. Are you trying to find a job by searching the "Help Wanted" ads, surfing the online job sites, searching company web sites and responding to their so-called "open positions," working with headhunters, and posting your resume on job boards? Unfortunately, those ways of finding a job are hopelessly ineffective.

Here's a little secret. According to parallel studies by a Harvard professor and the U.S. Department of Labor, the job market consists of two categories. The formal or "published" job market includes only 25 percent of the jobs that are available at any time. The informal or "unpublished" market is where the remaining 75 percent of the jobs that actually change hands are hidden. Both studies conclude that the best way to uncover the enormous unpublished job market is to start with the people that you know. Most outplacement services consultants tell their candidates that the most likely way to find their next job is through networking.

The fact is, in addition to using the conventional job-searching methods, your instincts have already told you that you should be working your network of contacts to help you find your next job. But for some reason it's not working out as well as you thought it would. Don't despair! Your instincts were right. You *should* be working on your contacts. You were just not working your network properly.

You were doing old networking. Old networking was when people tried to stay in touch with their collection of random contacts, built on a wide set of loose criteria—you liked someone, someone was a friend of a friend, or you met someone at a party. Believing that such a network was going to get you a job was an exercise in invalidated hope. Networking to get names was an exercise in futility. But networking with a purpose will position you to effectively contact the "right" person.

Knowing how to articulate exactly what you want this person to do for you will bring your network to life.

Tighten Your Seat Belt

By picking up this book, you are ready to go against the grain and differentiate yourself by employing your SuperNetwork—an intentional network-focused, actively-managed system, with work to do and results that are constantly measured. *SuperNetworking* will show you how to transform the usual circle of friends and contacts that most people think of as their "network" into something radically different. A SuperNetwork is a purpose-built machine for reaching out to specifically targeted people for a specific reason. With goals clearly in mind, a SuperNetwork inevitably gets you where you want to go, one sure step at a time.

SuperNetworking takes advantage of the breakthrough in network theory described in Macolm Gladwell's *The Tipping Point,* and Albert-Laslo Barabasi's *Linked: The New Science of Networks*. These books have shown that the famous distance of six degrees of separation is, in fact, much greater than the distance we really need to go to be able to surround and capture our target goals. *SuperNetworking* is the first method to take advantage of this new knowledge and transform the concept of networking from being something vague and arbitrary to becoming a system that is swift, deliberate, and effective.

Using *SuperNetworking* as a tool for finding a job will give you a powerful, fast-acting system that chooses target companies and people, builds powerful links that reach out to those companies and people, and radically shortens the process for achieving the specific goal. SuperNetworking gets you your job in days and weeks instead of months and years.

Unique to *SuperNetworking* are the concepts of choosing who is in your network, extracting promises from the people in your network, establishing a mechanism to track your progress and results, the critical role of a mentor in the networking process, and setting standards that will facilitate finding a new job in less time.

Have you ever heard the expression, "It's not what you know, but who you know"? It's true. A "cold call" hardly ever gets heard or returned. According to *Sales Management* magazine "warm calls" have a 90-percent response rate, and "cold calls" have a less than 10-percent response rate. Referrals will help you open doors you could not open on your own. This book will show you how to use the "warm call," a door opener that will increase your chances of getting your voice heard.

How to Use This Book

SuperNetworking will provide you with a complete, simple, practical, easy-to-follow, methodical, pro-active break-through system to access your current and future contacts to develop your career opportunities. The book is in a building-block format, with close connections between each chapter. Finally, *SuperNetworking* reveals how to build on the power of SuperNetworking to create a life of success, meaning, and accomplishment. The program will work for you, provided you are willing to get a mentor and do the work. There are no shortcuts to success. It's hard work, but the payoff is worth it.

I want to take a moment to tell you about Hank, a technical support professional who was recently laid off from a dot-com that didn't make it. Finding a similar position in Massachusetts was challenging, and Hank had a few obstacles to overcome. He was in his late 40s and was competing with people in their 20s to 30s. His salary requirements were greater than his competition's. Nevertheless, he followed the *SuperNetworking* program and landed a new job for more money in four weeks.

Here's what he had to say:

"The *SuperNetworking* program provided me with a focus and direction which made finding my new job a proactive and positive experience. The real value is that I was in control of everything and have a strategy for keeping track of my personal network of contacts."

You too can be like Hank. As the movie director Spike Lee said, "There is no such thing as an overnight success." People say you get what you deserve in life. I believe you get what you earn. If you don't want to be like everyone else, you will implement what you read in this book. To get the best results, you must have a plan, because if you don't know where you are going, all roads will lead you there. This book gives you that plan, step-by-step. The book will suggest *what* to do, but more importantly, will show you *how* to do it. By the end of the book, you will have developed the necessary ingredients and gained the know-how to differentiate yourself and increase your chances of finding your next job opportunity in an accelerated time frame.

All the Steps in Your Journey

In Chapter 1, you are going to learn the value of being organized, and work on a self-analysis and your elevator pitch. The self-analysis will help you choose a career direction or career focus, and help you clarify what you want to do next. The answers to these questions will become your personal profile, which will be used throughout the book. Also, you will learn how to put together an effective elevator pitch, which you will apply to what you've learned in the self-analysis. This pitch is your 20- to 30-second speech aimed to capture your audience's attention and articulate what that person would need to know in order to help you find a new job.

In Chapter 2, you are going to learn how to qualify personal and professional contacts by order of importance and categorize them appropriately. You will also learn how to use those contacts to find more contacts, increasing the number of people on your list. You will also be given a format to organize your contact list and have a repository in which to store your networking information.

In Chapter 3, you are going to realize the value of making a favorable impression by preparing for your phone calls. You will learn how to gather critical information about individuals and companies, and where to get it. You will also review a series of questions that will help you to discover your potential value in your targeted company. Most people just wing it and hope for the best. They generally fail. You are going to get one shot to make a strong impression with your contacts; successful preparation for the call will bring you closer to your new job.

In Chapter 4, you will learn how not to just spin your wheels, but how to create an effective road map to ensure that you reach your objective for every call you make. You will learn how to use the "warm call" to your advantage, find out what it means to "peel the onion" where you may have to go through numerous layers until you get to the core, find the "right" person that can help you, and highlight the key factors involved in establishing and maintaining your credibility.

You will be given a detailed example to help you put together a strategy. It will explain how to set call objectives, how to ask difficult questions, and the importance of "not letting people off the hook," but of getting a promise to act. It includes a thorough guide of helpful "do's and don'ts," as well as other helpful phone tips, and explains how to do a post-call debriefing, and the importance of a timely follow up and follow through.

In Chapter 5, you will learn how to create and use a call script which will be developed from the work you did in prior chapters, formulating your self-analysis, elevator pitch, due diligence, strategy, and call objective. Sample time-tested scripts and techniques will be provided to help you prepare your own. (I told you it would be hard work, remember? If you do the work exactly as I describe it, you will move forward quickly, increasing your network, and bringing you closer to finding your next job fast. The pay off is worth it.)

You will learn what to say and how to ask for help when speaking to your contacts and referrals. You will also learn how to leave effective voice mail messages that will be returned, and how to handle situations when someone gives you the "cold shoulder."

In Chapter 6, you will learn why this plan will not work if you don't report your progress to someone. If your boss told you to have a report on his desk by 5 p.m. tomorrow, would you produce it on time? Of course you would! If you imposed the same deadline on yourself, would you produce it on time? Maybe you would, maybe you wouldn't. In order for you to succeed in implementing this networking program, you must have a mentor who will help formalize the process, monitor your progress, and ensure that you stay focused until you have landed your new job.

After you launch your SuperNetworking plan you will become so busy with making phone calls, sending e-mails, scheduling interviews, and mailing resumes and follow-ups that can cause you to lose focus and effectiveness. You don't want things to start "slipping through the cracks." Most plans, such as diets, fail because, even though you start out with good intentions, you can become distracted and start to rationalize why you stopped. You will learn why it's important to only have one person to whom you report, how to select the best person for you, why you need to meet with them on a weekly basis, and how having this person can keep you on track and provide valuable support.

In Chapter 7, you will learn how to build a network database for getting a new job and for maintaining a network for life. This database will provide a constant progress report that will become the framework for the weekly discussions with your mentor. You need a place to keep track of what is said and what action needs to take place. This is critical to the plan. You will be given a sample progress report with set standards for "unacceptable, acceptable, and exceptional performance," which will provide a reality check for where you are relative to your goals and objectives. For example, some of the items that are tracked include interviews scheduled, resumes sent, phone calls made, and new contacts established.

In Chapter 8, you will learn how to find out as much as you can about a company and its hiring manager, how to identify and respond to "hot buttons" and create "killer" customized resumes and cover letters that will get your target audience's attention. You will be able to review time-tested samples that are action oriented, and easy to read, with distinguishing personal, professional, and performance accomplishments that pursuade people to go out of their way to help.

In Chapter 9, you will learn about the interview process. You will gain insight about how much emphasis companies place on candidates' ability, interpersonal "chemistry" and "fit" with the organization. You will also learn how critical it is to prepare properly for interviews, and what you should do in order to be ready.

During the interview process, you will probably encounter people in a variety of positions on the organizational chart, such as human resources, senior managers, direct reports, and financial managers. You will learn about each of these groups, the roles they are likely to play in the hiring process, and how to speak to them by understanding their "hot buttons." You will also learn what types of questions to ask, how to ask them, and the do's and don'ts of how to make a favorable impression, including what to wear.

In Chapter 10, you will be shown a decision-making tree that will show you all the options at each stage of the salary negotiating process. You will learn how to evaluate the job offer regarding environment, long-range opportunity, your role and responsibilities, the company's viability, salary, benefits, and the value proposition. You will be shown a step-by-step process of how to navigate your way through the negotiation process to ensure a win-win outcome.

By Chapter 11—congratulations! You made it! You got the job! But you have accomplished more that that. The job was just the by-product of the work that you did and the new skill you developed—the art of SuperNetworking. (The appendix supplies you with additional worksheets for all of the exercises found throughout *SuperNetworking*. You can photocopy them to use as often as you need.)

You will take a long look forward and learn the importance of constantly updating your contact list and keeping it fresh. You will learn why this is just the beginning of a lifetime process of SuperNetworking. You will learn what you have to do to treat your network as you would a treasure, which needs to be nourished, preserved, and developed.

You will learn that networking is a two-way street of giving and receiving. At the beginning of this process you were the beneficiary of help from others. Once you've gotten the job you wanted, it's important not to forget what others did to help you. You will now be in a position to return the favor and help others. That's part of the deal. It's an unwritten understanding that you will help others. *You* are now going to be the one giving advice, or allowing others to use your name to open up a door. You are going to make yourself known as a resource, a Center of Influence (COI).

Take a Deep Breath

This book is designed in a positive, supportive style that should make it easy for you to follow the process. Over the years, I have worked with countless job seekers and feel I know what it's like to be in your shoes. Because of my experience, I have plenty of sympathy for what you are going through. In this book I'll be standing right next to you, offering immediate, practical solutions to all of your job seeking problems.

To reach the results you want, you must have a plan. John Wooden, the most successful coach in college basketball, said "Failing to prepare is preparing to fail." Wooden knows what he is talking about. His record includes a .804 winning percentage over a 23-year period and won a record 10 NCAA championships, including seven in a row from 1966–1973 at UCLA. He may have lost a few games, but he always walked into the arena with a well-thought-out game plan. In order to be a winner, you need to be ready to plan the work and work the plan.

Are you ready to go against the grain, separate yourself from the pack, and get back to work faster? If you follow the plan as outlined in this book, you will find your next job in an accelerated time frame. Even better, the next time you are in position of needing a new job, you will not have to look so far or work so hard to make your next big step. Your next opportunity will be right there in your SuperNetwork.

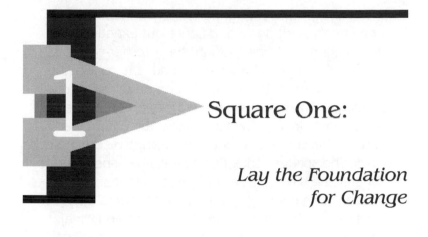

Square One:

Lay the Foundation for Change

You are about to look for your next job opportunity, but you don't know where to begin. You are thinking of calling people you know, responding to job postings, and contacting some headhunters. You are not quite sure of the best way to approach the job market.

You need a plan that will provide you with:

> Focus.

> Purpose.

> Strategy.

> Tactics.

> Results.

Rebecca put the "jobs" section of the Sunday newspaper down and began thinking about how to start her job search. "None of the ads under Marketing look interesting," she thought to herself. "And anyway, first I need to sit down and figure out exactly what I am looking for." She thought back to her previous jobs—what part of each one had she loved the most? She really loved working on developing new products. And because she had lots of contacts and experience in the food industry, this was clearly where she could leverage her strengths. But how could she spark a contact's interest when she called? What if she said, "Hi, I am Rebecca Jacobsen, and I wrote the marketing plan for new products that re-vitalized the frozen foods division of your major competitor. I want to talk with you about what I can do for your business."

Do you think she has a legitimate chance of getting her foot in the door? Of course she does. She has determined that by taking a more focused approach, she will get closer to her desired goal. Most people take the opposite approach. They don't want to be "pigeon holed" and are concerned that if they are too narrow in their search they will miss out on opportunities. They want to use a broad approach and cast out the nets and see what may come in. The reality is, very little will come in. The people who are trying to fill job openings do not pore over hundreds of resumes trying to discern whether or not the applicant fits the job. People trying to fill job openings are *not* going to define you. You must define yourself and make it clear who you are to others.

Self-Analysis

The first step in your journey is getting to know yourself. You need to be clear about what you're good at, determine where your passion lies, and understand what will truly make you happy. To do this, you must quantify your personal and professional strengths and learn how to clearly articulate your talents.

Knowing yourself and being able to clearly communicate who you are is a core competency that will prepare you for future conversations and meetings with your contacts and referrals.

You are in a competition, whether you know it or not

Jobs are not simply opportunities that are open and that you have a chance to fill. The moment a job comes into existence, a competition opens up for that job. People inside the organization may want the job. Friends of friends will hear about the job. Ads will run, and dozens and even hundreds of applicants will want that job.

Jobs are competitive. You need to think about your competition all the time. You will need to be better than them, stand out, and clearly be seen as the best candidate for the position.

Being able to clearly articulate your strengths and communicate exactly what you want in your next job opportunity will separate you from your competition. Your competition generally lacks that focus when pursuing their next career move.

As you begin SuperNetworking, be confident that this journey will get you to your destination. It's important that you enjoy the journey because you are going to find opportunities along the way, possibly in places you hadn't imagined. As one door you thought would be open closes, another one will present itself to you. You need to be ready to walk right through it. You are about to develop new relationships that will help you and, as of now, you don't really know where many of those relationships will be coming from. That's life. Life is what happens in between your plans. So be ready.

What you need to do now is get ready to put pen to paper and complete a self-analysis. The answers to these questions will become your personal profile, which you will often refer back to in subsequent chapters. Completing the self-analysis will help you choose a career direction or focus, and help you clarify what you want to do next.

We will be using examples of people doing their self-analysis. You can use them as a reference while you complete your own. Meet Lucy and Mark. Lucy is a technical writer and Mark is a sales executive.

This is step one of the building block process. Let's get to work.

Self-analysis #1:
Lucy, technical writer

Part I

What I am good at?

My strengths include writing, creating, and organizing information to develop instructional materials.

What is my area of expertise?

Business knowledge to develop instructional materials for the financial industry.

What and where is my passion?

Developing training programs and writing.

What will make me happy?

Developing and implementing a training program.

What is my value to an organization?

My experience in the financial services industry and in developing training.

Where is my value to an organization?

As a senior-level training specialist designing curriculum to meet the needs of the target audience, determining where training gaps exist, and implementing a training program to meet the need.

What should people know about me professionally?

I am respectful, loyal, trustworthy, hardworking, and will give a company my "all" on any necessary projects. I enjoy learning new things and sharing my knowledge with others.

What should people know about me personally?

I tend to be very driven when working on a project, but ultimately require a balance between my personal and professional life to remain productive. In my free time I enjoy reading, biking, and cooking.

How have I "wowed" companies in the past?

An opportunity to develop and deliver a 2-day training session from the ground up targeting 50 regional vice presidents was presented a few years ago. Six coworkers and I worked to develop and present the training within an 18-day window. This meant undergoing a "train the trainer" session to gain understanding of a CRM application for which we were to develop the training, determine curriculum and training needs, develop supporting training documentation (including manuals and job aids, slides, presentational props and participatory activities), and assist the IT division to ensure that all equipment was in working order. The training was successfully implemented and our team was used as a resource to prepare future follow-up training sessions.

What would my manager say about me?

Lucy is very loyal, dedicated, and hardworking. She adapts easily to a changing environment and is always willing to take on and/or help with projects at the drop of a hat. She is easy to work with, very focused, and detail oriented. Her dedication and focus allow her to complete projects in a timely manner.

What am I looking for in my next opportunity?

I am looking for a challenging position that will allow me to develop and implement an instructional design program.

Part II

What's the size of the company I would like to work for, in terms of revenue and people?

I would like to work for a company with no more than 500 employees and annual revenue of more that $150 million.

Do I want to be with a publicly-held or privately-held company?

I want to be with a publicly-held company.

Do I want to work in a start-up situation, early-stage company, or an established company?

The company should be well established and exhibit steady growth.

In what type of business would the company be?

Because of my extensive background in the financial services industry, I would prefer to work for an investment management, banking, brokerage firm or a consulting organization targeting the financial services industry.

What kind of corporate culture do I prefer? (formal, informal, virtual/work at home)

The corporate culture should be one where respect for and among all employees exists. Managers should remain open to new ideas and understand the need for continuing employee growth and education.

What's kind of work environment do I prefer?

The environment should be laid back and have a casual business dress code.

For how long do I want to commute every day?

I want my commute to be no longer than 30 to 45 minutes.

Where would I prefer my company be located? Do I want to be in the city or suburbs?

I want the company to be in the city because I would like to take advantage of public transportation. However, I would consider driving to a company provided the drive would be no longer than 45 minutes, and the corporate policy allowed flexibility in working from home.

Do I want to travel?

I would want my job to consist of no more than 25 percent travel.

SELF-ANALYSIS #2:
MARK, SALES AND MARKETING EXECUTIVE

Part I

What I am good at?

Sales and marketing in the service business. Driving revenue and profits.

What is my area of expertise?

Sales and marketing management, working through other people. An ability to develop and execute plans, strategic thinker.

What and where is my passion?

Managing, mentoring, and training people. Creating the vision, working on big picture opportunities, being the architect of the future development of the long-term strategy.

What will make me happy?

Either running a marketing or sales organization, or both.

What is my value to an organization?

My years of experience with a proven track record.

Where is my value to an organization?

I am a senior level management position driving revenues and profits, exceeding expectations; developing corporate identity programs, my understanding of

how sales and marketing need to work "hand in glove."
I am a strategic thinker contributing to the development of the organization's long-term strategy.

What should people know about me professionally?

I am results oriented. I deliver what I promise. I have a
demonstrated track record of increasing revenue and
profitability in every organization for which I have
worked. I am organized and methodical in my thinking,
I lead by example. I am a good listener, have excellent
communication and planning skills, am a serious, highly
focused team player.

What should people know about me personally?

I am passionate, hardworking, dedicated, loyal, committed, honest, and very direct. I enjoy sharing my
knowledge with others, and strive to find more balance in my life. My family is very important to me.
In addition, I have always been involved in team and
individual sports.

How have I "wowed" companies in the past?

One example: During the last recession 10 years ago,
I joined a service company with revenues of $50 mil-
lion and Gross Profit Margin (GP) of 12 percent. In
addition, we closed only 23 percent of all proposals
submitted. Within two years, we increased revenue
to $80 million and increased GP Margin to 20 per-
cent, and we closed 53 percent of all proposals submitted. We did it by educating our managers on
creating value in their relationships to drive GP with
their current accounts, dropping lower margin accounts, educating and training the sales staff on how
to sell using the "conceptual and strategic" selling

methodology, doing a better job of qualifying opportunities, and selling more on value rather than price.

What would my manager say about me?

The most highly focused executive that they have ever worked with. Mark is knowledgeable, dedicated, hardworking, loyal, passionate, and reliable. He does not require a lot of my time. He knows what needs to be done and he executes. He is a valued member of the management team because he is well versed in all aspects of business. He understands numbers, is bottom-line oriented, knows how to sell, is likeable, personable, and not afraid to speak his mind.

What I am looking for in my next opportunity?

A challenge. I am interested in getting equity, and finding a place where I can stay for a long time.

Part II

Now that you have a good idea about your field of knowledge and your transferable skills, you must answer some additional questions about the type of company you want to work for.

What's the size of the company in revenue and people?

I'd like to work for a company that has between $50–$100M in annual revenue and 100–150 people in the corporate offices.

Do I want to be with a publicly-held or privately-held company?

I'd like to work for a privately held company and possibly get equity.

Do I want to work in a start-up situation, early stage company, or established company?

I do not want to work in a start-up, as it is too risky. I want a company that has a track record and has been in business for at least three years.

In what type of business (for example, high-tech, financial services, manufacturing) would the company be?

I want to remain in the service business.

What's the culture like (formal, informal, virtual/work at home)?

I want a culture where everybody is committed to success. Where everyone is treated with respect and follows the golden rule. Also, that they are not "clock watchers" and a place where you are evaluated by the results.

What's environment do I prefer?

Casual environment. I do not want to go back to the shirt and tie routine.

For how long do I want to commute everyday?

It's not critical, but I'd like to keep my drive to one hour each way.

Where is the company located? Do I want to be in the city or suburbs?

It's a non-issue.

Do I want to travel?

Up to 50 percent, no more.

STEP 1: SELF-ANALYSIS

(WRITE YOUR ANSWERS IN THE SPACES PROVIDED)

Part I

What am I good at?

_____

_____

_____

What is my area of expertise?

_____

_____

What and where is my passion?

_____

_____

_____

What will make me happy?

_____

_____

_____

What is my value to an organization?

_____

_____

_____

_____

_____

_____

_____

Where is my value to an organization?

_____

_____

_____

_____

_____

_____

_____

_____

What should people know about me professionally?

_____

_____

_____

_____

_____

_____

_____

What should people know about me personally?

_____

_____

_____

_____

_____

_____

_____

How have I "wowed" companies in the past?

_____

_____

_____

_____

_____

What would my manager say about me?

_____

_____

_____

_____

What I am looking for in my next opportunity?

_____

_____

_____

Part II

Now that you have a good idea about your field of knowledge and your transferable skills, you must answer some additional questions about the type of company you want to work for.

What's the size of the company in revenue and people?

_____

_____

Do I want to be with a publicly-held or privately-held company?

_____

_____

Do I want to work in a start-up situation, early-stage company, or an established company?

_____

_____

In what type of business (high-tech, financial services, manufacturing, advertising) would the company be?

_____

_____

What's kind of corporate culture do I prefer (formal, informal, virtual/work at home)?

_____

_____

What's kind of environment do I prefer?

_____

_____

_____

_____

For how long will I commute everyday?

_____

_____

Where is the company located? Do I want to be in the city or suburbs?

_____

_____

Do I want to travel?

_____

Have you ever been talking to someone and it sounded so canned, robotic, or boring that it seemed it really didn't matter whether you were there? Have you ever held the phone away from your ear because the person on the other line was just rambling, and when you came back to phone the person was still rambling? Or someone is talking to you in person and you start to "zone out" because they are boring you to tears? Obviously these people had no idea you were turned off and were not paying attention because they kept on talking. Do not let yourself become this person. That's why we are going to work on your articulation, or elevator pitch.

You are going to develop your elevator pitch in which you will apply what you have learned about yourself in your self-analysis. If you haven't finished your self-analysis, now is a good time to do it.

Elevator Pitch

An elevator pitch is a 30- to 45- second speech designed to capture your target audience's interest and attention. After that time period, you've either got them or lost them.

In this pitch, you will aim to capture another person's interest within 45 seconds and articulate what that person would need to know about you in order to help you find your next job opportunity.

This pitch is used in many situations: on the phone talking to contacts and referrals; meeting people in the grocery store; or running into someone at a local soccer game, dinner party, wedding, conference, luncheon, or any other public venue.

You need to make sure that your pitch is focused, not broad. The elements of an effective pitch incorporate:

➤ Clearly articulating the talents that you want someone to know you possess.

➤ Making it easy for people to understand by using simple language, and not using language that is too technical.

➤ Having an objective. What do you want to accomplish during this conversation?

Here are a few sample pitches that will help you to prepare your own. In some situations you will find yourself strictly talking business, in others strictly pleasure, and then sometimes you will mix both. It's a fine line, and you don't want to overstep your boundaries in that type of scenario. The scripts you will read will serve more as a guideline than the rule. After looking at these scripts, you will need to create a few "elevator pitches" that make sense to you, and ones that you will feel comfortable with. You need to incorporate your personality with what you create so that it appears believable and credible.

Situation 1: Lucy, the Technical Writer, is at a PTO meeting at her daughter's school. She is sitting next to a friend she hasn't seen in a few months. They've never really discussed their professional lives.

Lucy is currently employed, but looking for a new opportunity and decides to speak to her friend about her circumstances. They have already finished up the pleasantries and small talk.

"Jenna, during the last 5 years, I have worked in the financial services industry in various capacities, including service, communications, and training. My interests lie in developing training and I am looking for a position as a training designer in my industry. Do you know anyone that works in the financial service field I can speak to?"

What did you think? It was clear, concise, and easy to understand. You knew what she wanted to do, and she also made it easy for Jenna to think about whom she may know in the financial services industry. Most people are too broad and may ask, "Do you know of any opportunities?" or, "Do you know anyone hiring?" Don't make that mistake.

Situation 2: Frank, a software developer was recently "downsized" from a medium-sized, high technology company. He is attending a "pink slip" networking meeting where everyone gets a chance to exchange leads.

> "Hi, I am Frank Peters. I have been a software engineer for 10 years. I love working in technology. I worked with JAVA when people thought it was coffee. I was a paper millionaire but never had a payday. I've worked in start-ups and mid-sized firms, mostly in manufacturing, pharmaceutical, and technology. I am in transition now and I want to find a position locally with a company in either of those industries. Can you help me?"

What did you think about this one? Frank gave his target audience an excellent mental picture of what he's done. When he said "I love technology," you got to really feel his passion. Also, by mentioning that he "was a paper millionaire, but never had a payday" shows a little humility and part of his personality was coming through. Lastly, he mentioned he wants to stay local, and identified three industries he is interested in. Again, this is good because he was very specific and made it easy for his target audience to think of anyone they know in those industries whom Frank may be able to call.

Notice how Frank handled the fact that he had been "downsized." He said, "I am in transition." He did not explain what happened. *You* don't have to either. If people ask why you're looking for a job, be honest with them. But don't feel obligated to explain. Another possible statement that works well in your pitch is "I'm actively looking."

Obviously there is more to say when you are having a lengthy conversation. This is just for your pitch. We will cover what to say and how to say it during your conversations with contacts and referrals in Chapter 5.

Situation 3: Marty, a sales representative, is at the wedding of his wife's best friend. Marty has been out of work for two months. He wants to make contacts, but also doesn't want to appear desperate to the guests at the wedding. Here are two types of approaches he can use to help "break the ice."

Option A

"Hi, I'm Marty Saunders. My wife happens to be Kaye's best friend. I live nearby on Chestnut. We've got two kids, 10 and 15 years old, and my greatest joy is spending time with them—especially watching them on the athletic field. How about you? Are you married? Do you have any kids?"

In this scenario Marty didn't talk about his work. He gave his target audience a nice picture of who he is personally. Then, he asked a question which could lead to additional dialogue. Even though Marty didn't talk about himself professionally he still had all the key elements in his pitch. He told the target audience something about himself that he wanted to get across. It was easy to follow, and he had an objective—find out about the target audience by taking the personal approach.

Option B

"Hi, I am Marty Saunders. My wife is Kaye's best friend. What's your connection here?"

After Marty g_ts a response from his "break the ice question," he continues with:

"What do you do for a living?"

In this more basic scenario, Marty got into the conversation casually. He introduced himself in a gentle, social way followed by a subtle probing question to see if there might be a connection. Depending on how it goes, this type of approach gives you an opportunity to engage in a more lengthy dialogue introducing your elevator pitch at the appropriate time.

"My background is sales in the insurance industry working with mostly property and casualty firms."

Here he gave his target audience a condensed version of his background. Again, it was simple, easy to understand, and he turned it around with a probing question to find out more about this person. Nice going, Marty.

Articulation

Record the main points you want to use in your pitch and create a script that effectively articulates your talents. Remember to reference your self-analysis (pages 33-39). Here a few other things to consider when preparing your pitch:

What am I most proficient in?

_____

_____

What makes me stand out from the pack?

_____

_____

How have I "wowed" companies in the past?

_____

_____

_____

What do I "bring to the table?"

_____

_____

_____

What's important to my target audience?

_____

_____

_____

You will find that you probably will be customizing different pitches as things develop.

Congratulations, you are out of the gate. I told you it would require some work on your part, but now you are on your way. Let's make sure you are ready to go forward.

Read through this checklist and see if you can put a check next to every statement. If you can do that, saying yes to each of these questions, you are ready to proceed to Chapter 2. If not, you need to go back and complete the exercises. Remember, the program has a building-block approach. You can't shortcut the process. It's like building a house. It needs to have a solid foundation and be built brick-by-brick.

Square One Checklist

❏ I have completed my self-analysis.

❏ I now have a focus, or a better idea of what I want do next.

❏ I now know the importance of having an effective elevator pitch.

❏ I have created my own elevator pitch that articulates an objective and articulates what my target audience needs to know to help me.

You are starting to get clarity and focus about finding your next job opportunity. That's good because most people are "all over the map" and very vague. You are not. Let's move on.

Six Degrees of Separation:

Build A Network of Contacts and Referrals

Barry, an introverted engineer, had been mulling over how he was going to use networking to get a job. He was not the type of person who made friends easily, and he wasn't sure if he knew anyone who had any influence or who would be able to help him. Then it suddenly occurred to him that he did have contacts—he had accumulated plenty of business cards from customers and vendors during his years in the aerospace industry. He just hadn't thought of those people as a "network" before. He thought, "Maybe this will work!" He hurried to his computer to start organizing their names into lists.

Everyone has a network. Whether you have contact information stored in your head, a shoebox of cards, a Rolodex, PalmPilot, or telephone book, you know people. You just have to think about it. For some, the list could be in the hundreds and for others, fewer. In the movie *Field of Dreams*, Kevin Costner kept waking up from a deep sleep because he heard the words *if you build it, they will come*. You need to build your list properly and then your contacts will help you get to the right person that can help you.

You need to create your contact list. Then you will be shown how to categorize and manage this list appropriately.

Who Should Be on Your List?

Do not put just anybody on this list. What you have to do now is start thinking about the people who can and will help you find the job you want based on where you want to work next (based on the self-analysis you completed).

➤ **Family.** Don't just think of immediate family. Think of your extended family—your brother-in-law's sister and your distant cousins.

➤ **Close friends.** These are the people you are close to, whose friendships you value. These are people you can always count on.

➤ **People you know through others.** People that didn't make your "close friend" list. They are people you are friendly with, and whom you feel comfortable asking for a favor.

➤ **Customers.** People you have done business with. Over time, you have established a good rapport with each of these people. You would feel comfortable calling any of them for a favor, and feel confident they would give you a positive response.

➤ **Prospects.** These are people whom you have never done business with, but over time, you have developed and maintained some sort of relationship with. Even though you haven't done business with them, there is mutual respect. You may have similar interests, such as sports, or you have some things in common, such as having kids the same age.

➤ **Vendors.** These are people whom you know because their company provided service to you and companies you have worked with. Some of these people could be your printer, advertising company, search/staffing firm, and security or cleaning firm.

➤ **Association and club members.** These are people whom you know through trade-related associations, chamber of commerce, golf, tennis, or swim clubs, local PTO, Mason, or Rotary.

➤ **Professional contacts.** These are people you have developed excellent professional relationships with, but have never really established a personal one. They could also be people you are working with, or have worked with in the past. These are people whom you know through associations, or from conferences you have gone to over the years.

➤ **Competitors.** These are also people you know through business. Just as many lawyers know each other, you probably have met people in your field that work for your competition. Do you think they may be a good source to get you closer to your next opportunity? Of course they are.

The conversations you will have with people on your list will be slightly different depending on the type of relationship you have with that individual. The way you speak, what you say, and the type of intimate details you share regarding your current situation will vary. What you tell your brother will be different from what you would say to a vendor. That is why you need to categorize this contact list appropriately into four different levels of contacts—A, B, C, and D. Organizing it makes it easy to maneuver.

Categorize Your Contact List

Your **"A" List** should consist of at least 10 people you consider "heavy hitters," or "well connected." These are people you think are powerful in their business area. These people are ones you think can "make things happen" by making a phone call on your behalf. These people come from any one of the lists above. They could be a business owner, president, CEO, CFO, COO, vice president, or other high visibility/high profile personality.

Your **"B" List** should consist of at least 10 people from your family, close friends, and people you know through other lists. These are people you can have candid conversations with and whom you know you can rely upon.

Your **"C" List** should consist of at least 10 people you know from your people you know through others, customers, prospects, vendors, associations and clubs, professional contacts, and competitors lists. In addition, add to this list your lawyer, doctor, accountant, stockbroker, and your life insurance salesperson. Consider how many business people they know. I am confident they can help you, too.

Your **"D" List** should consist of at least 10 people you wouldn't at first think would be people who could help you. This might sound odd at first but your "D" list people are those who are not particularly powerful, but who might know the "right" person you are looking for. These highly connected "D" list people could be your physical therapist, dry cleaner, butcher, or tailor. Let's take your physical therapist as an example:

Your physical therapist works with people recovering from injuries and surgery. On average, they spend 30 minutes with a patient, meeting approximately 80 people per week. What do you think people talk to their physical therapist about? Generally people talk about their families, what's going on with their life, and work. Can you imagine how many professionals this person knows? Do you think this person would refer you to someone if they knew what you were looking for? You bet!

My tailor, Benny, used to work for a fine men's clothing store. Ten years ago he went out on his own and his customers followed. His business has grown and he has an unparalleled reputation in the city of Boston. Benny's clients are predominately senior level people in different industries from financial services to hospitality, from entertainment to biotechnology. One day, Benny showed me his Rolodex. It was a who's who of the Boston business community. If I were looking for a job in the financial services industry, I would call Benny before I would call anyone on my "A" list. People we don't often think of as a possible link can be an unexpected and invaluable resource.

Create a list of contacts and categorize them using the Contact List Template on page 52.

Now that you have a clear focus, an effective elevator pitch, and a comprehensive list of contacts, you are getting closer to

CONTACT LIST

"A" List	"B" List	"C" List	"D" List

the right person with whom to speak. In fact, you are probably closer than you imagined and you must simply think of building your SuperNetwork in terms of making the right connection.

6 Degrees of Separation

It has been demonstrated that we are all six people removed from anyone else in the universe. That means that if you want to reach someone you don't yet know, you can do it by building the missing connections in your network to that person. These connections are built in two directions at once—from you to your target, and from the target back to you. For instance, if you are trying the reach the CEO of a company, you can research her bio, find what business school she attended, and go through your contacts until you find someone you know who went to the same business school. You are now just two degrees from the person you are trying to reach. How you close that gap is one of key secrets of SuperNetworking, and you will learn to master it in later chapters.

Using your SuperNetwork of contacts, you will soon find that you have access to people you never thought you would have.

I was conducting a workshop for BrassRing in Santa Clara, California where I explained this concept to a large group of unemployed Information Technology professionals. I told them that through my network of contacts, I was six degrees of separation from anyone I wanted to access, and they were too. One participant raised their hand and challenged me to see if I could access Carli Fiorina, Chairman and Chief Executive Officer of Hewlett-Packard. There was a hush in the audience waiting for the moment of truth. I thought about it for a few minutes and told this student, "I can access Carli Fiorina in three phone calls. In my previous life in executive searching, we placed IT professionals for Hewlett-Packard Consulting's Northeast Business Unit. Their consulting practice was HP's most profitable line of business. My contact was a Vice President and had Profit and Loss responsibility for the business unit. Because Ms. Fiorina is focused on the bottom line and this business unit was a large contributor, I am confident that a contact could be established. My call to my contact would be the first call. His call would be to his boss. That would be the second call. His boss reports directly to Ms. Fiorina. His boss calling Ms. Fiorina would be the third call."

At another workshop I conducted for the St. John's University Men's Basketball program in Jamaica, New York, a similar challenge was given to me. This student wanted to know if I could access basketball superstar Michael Jordan. I told him I could make that happen in two phone calls. Their head coach, Mike Jarvis, is a friend of mine. Three years ago, when Michael Jordan was in one of his retirement phases, he was the President of the Washington Wizards. Michael Jordan recruited Mike Jarvis to become the head coach for the Wizards. Even though Mike Jarvis did not take the job, they still know each other. My first phone call would be to Mike Jarvis. The second call would be Mike calling Michael Jordan on my behalf.

I really do not have an interest in speaking to either Carli Fiorina or Michael Jordan. However, this is more a reflection of the power of my *SuperNetwork* that I can access people or information easier and faster. You can accomplish the same results if you put your mind to it. Whether it's targeting a company or person, start thinking about who in your network you know might be able to get you started in the right direction.

Recently, I was in Connecticut conducting a workshop for a group that was being downsized by a multi-national manufacturing company. One individual, William, was the plant's environmental engineer. He said he was having a hard time finding a new position because there were not many manufacturing companies left in Southern Connecticut. I asked him if any of the local towns or cities would have a need for someone with his skills. He said yes and that he would be interested in pursuing an opportunity to work for a municipality, but he did not know where to begin.

He told me he lived in Redding, Connecticut and he knew his town manager. I suggested that he contact his town manager, let him know that he's interested in working for a municipality, and ask him if he might have an opportunity for him in Redding. If not, maybe he could either give him the names of other Town Managers he knew or could call them on William's behalf to see if he could make these people aware of his talent and availability.

Before we had this conversation, William thought he was at a dead end. After our conversation, William was eager to get on the phone and contact his friend the town manager. He was now working on a potential opportunity he had not before imagined he had.

There is no guarantee that William will get his new job through this contact. However, as he goes through the process, he is going to start increasing his network of contacts which may open up another door he was not counting on. Also, he now will have the knowledge of who these people are and what they do. In the future, he may have another opportunity to contact them for an entirely different opportunity, to seek advice, or gather information about their company.

The right person for you to contact is out there too. It is very possible that your contact will refer you to someone else. You may find that this contact or the person they told you to call may not be able to help you with a specific company or person. Either way, you need to capture that pertinent information because even though this person can't help you now, you may need their help at a later date. You just never know where your next opportunity is going to come from, and how many people you may have to contact to get there.

Organizing the People You Know

When you begin working this program, you are going to find yourself extremely busy calling people, sending resumes, scheduling meetings, going on interviews, and constantly adding to your network of contacts. You need to keep everything together in one place so you can be more efficient and effective with your time.

It is important to capture the pertinent information in one place. Without writing it down in an organized way, you'll cease to be effective and things will start to slip through the cracks. Having a contact form to use as a guideline will allow you to track and organize your contacts.

You need to treat every piece of information equally because you don't know which one could be the one that will point you toward success. You cannot afford to lose track of even one piece of information. Every lead, no matter how small or where it came from (and even though it may appear to be a long shot) must be treated with extreme care.

One summer, I was with three other guys going to the beach. I ran into a woman I knew that was there with two friends. She told us the beach was windy and asked if we wanted to join them at a pond close by. We ended up spending the day with them. As I tried to talk with one of the women during the day, I was picking up the vibe that she was not interested in me. As we were leaving the pond, her roommate asked if she could borrow my grill, and I said yes.

I went to their apartment later in the week to pick up the grill. The woman who gave me the cold shoulder was there. We talked for a few minutes and I asked her for a date. She accepted. We have been happily married for 20 years and have three children. If we had not met them that day and gone to the pond, my life would probably be different. You just never know when opportunity is knocking. Your next lead could be the one.

I do not recommend one database or another. Some people prefer to capture their information on an Excel spreadsheet. The sample format listed on pages 58 and 59 is a guideline for a repository to capture and store critical information you gather when adding to your network of contacts.

Defining the fields

→ **Contact.** This is a person that you know directly. and one that you have put on your contacts list because you have some type of relationship. Make sure you have the correct spelling for this person's name. Just because you know each other doesn't mean you have the right spelling.

→ **Phone Number.** Make sure it is correct. Attention to this type of detail is very important.

CONTACT FORM

Contact	Phone #	E-mail	Referral(s)	Company	Title, if known
Michael Satitz	(508) 555-0000	Msaltz@ msn.com	Lou Lazar	Eleco	President
			Carl Berklund	Myte Security	VP of Finance
			Karen Carlson	System Works	VP of Marketing

Contact Form (*continued*)

Referral's Phone & E-mail	Comments	Action to be taken	Date of Contact
(781) 555-0000 laze@eleco.com	Michael gave me three names. He's calling all three for me to set it up.	1. Call Michael next week to see if he got through to everyone. 2. Call his contacts on the 2nd.	July 12
(508) 555-0000			
(978) 555-0000			

➤ **E-mail.** There are many ways an e-mail can go wrong because of its set up. Be especially careful here.

➤ **Referral.** This is the person your contact told you to call. Here's an example: You called your contact, Michael Saltiz, and told him you were looking to get into the Eleco Company, and asked if he knew anyone there. He said his good friend,Lou Lazar worked there. Upon further dialogue he was able to give you two other referrals, Carl Berklund and Karen Carlson. Keeping track of these referrals is critical.

   If those referrals give you additional names, you would set up a place for their name in the contact field and the names they give you to contact get placed in the referral field.

➤ **Company.** This would be the company where your referral works.

➤ **Title, if known.** This would be the referral's title. You definitely want to get this information before you contact this individual.

➤ **Referral's phone number and e-mail address.** Please refer to what was mentioned previously for the phone number and e-mail field and follow the same guidelines when dealing with referrals.

➤ **Comments.** This is a very important field. You need to capture the essence of your conversation because, as you get busy, it will become almost impossible for you to remember every conversation you had. By capturing the information here, you will be able to refresh your memory and look at the chronology of all conversations you had with an individual. You need to develop the habit of making careful notes immediately after you hang up.

➤ **Action to be taken.** This field will let you keep track of your actions. By recording this information accurately, you will always know the status of your activity. If you are working your network of contacts correctly, every phone call or visit will trigger a future activity. As more activity and action take place, this field becomes especially important.

➤ **Date of initial contact.** It is important that you enter the date for every communication you have. You cannot possibly keep track of the status of all your activities in your head. Timing is crucial and you must be organized in that way.

Take your list of contacts and enter their essential information into the contact form (see pages 240-241).

Go through the following checklist and see if you can put a check next to every statement. If you can do that you are ready to proceed to Chapter 3. If not, you need to go back and complete the exercises.

❒ I have completed my list of contacts.

❒ I have categorized them appropriately into A, B, C, and D lists.

❒ I have taken the lists of A, B, C, and D and entered all of their essential information into the contact form.

Where You Are Now

1. You know what you want to do.

2. You have a strong "elevator pitch."

3. You know who you want to call.

Do you think you are ready to call them? You might think so, but you still have a little more "front end" work to do. It's time to learn about conducting the necessary prep work you need to do for your initial phone call.

Dynamite First Impressions:

Prepare for the Initial Contact

Shuana tapped her pen on the legal pad where she had just underlined "five years experience major auto accounts" on her list of strong points. Yes, that would be the clincher! She was finally ready to call her next contact, the creative director at an advertising agency with a high profile automotive client who was looking for more copy-writers. Shuana usually preferred to operate spon-taneously, rather than plan what she was going to say. But she could not just "wing it" with these calls—her chances of landing a better job depended on making a good impression. She had all the qualifications she needed, but knowing she could make a warm call was giving her that extra edge of confidence. Her previous networking had gotten her an introduction to Dana, who agreed to this set up. She began her call: "Hi, Dana. It's Shuana. You said to call you back today at this time. Is this still good for you?"

After they got the pleasantries out of the way, Shuana was able to set herself apart from her competition and demonstrate that she had done some homework on Dana's company by saying, "In the preliminary research I have done on your firm, it is my understanding you are looking for copywriters with major auto account experience. For the past three years, while working at the Lorenz agency, I wrote copy for The Auto Zone account." Do you think Shuana has a good chance of at least getting an interview with Dana to discuss her qualifications? Absolutely!

You need to prepare carefully for every one of your contact calls. Your contacts are pure gold and should not be squandered. People often assume that because contacts are close friends, they will go out of their way to help. This is not always the case.

Nick, a financial analyst was looking for a job. Jim was a vice president of taxes at a large organization, and someone Nick wanted to reach. Their mutual friend Steve told Nick to call Jim and use his name to "open the door." It worked. Nick got through to Jim quickly. Nick said, "Steve suggested I contact you. I'd like to send you my resume. Would that be okay?" And that's all he said. Because of the relationship Jim had with the mutual friend Steve, of course he said, "Sure. Send it." What do you think Jim did when the resume finally arrived? It went into the wastebasket. Nick had not made a good impression on Jim. He had squandered the opportunity of a warm call.

Here's a similar situation that had a different outcome: I received a call from Victoria, a woman who worked for me when I was in the executive search business. She recently completed a contract assignment and decided she wanted a position as a recruiter working for a corporation. She told me that she recently had seen a posting for a recruiting position with one of the world's largest office supply retailers.

She remembered that I used to do business with this firm and asked me if I still had any contacts there and, if so, if I would call on her behalf. I made the initial call. She followed up a day later, spoke to the hiring manager, and demonstrated her knowledge and understanding about his business and position. She was able to secure an interview for the following week.

Victoria had the same opportunity as Nick. I believe she was able to make the most of that phone call because of a few specific actions. She took what could have been a random response to a Web posting and used her network of contacts to open the door for her, which allowed her to separate herself from the pack and start at the top of the hundreds of responses that the hiring manager was going to receive for the job opening. Her investment in conducting some "front end" research work on the organization and the position, along with the probing she did with me to get a feeling about the personality of this individual, gave Victoria a sense of confidence when she made the initial call to the hiring manager.

What Nick should have done was be more articulate in giving Jim some direction on how he might help Nick in his efforts. Nick could have explained in more detail what type of situation he was seeking. He could have held Jim more accountable by asking him what he would do if he liked the resume, to whom it would be sent, and he could also have asked for the names and contact information of those people. He then would have found it appropriate to schedule a follow-up phone conversation with Jim to get a status report on any feedback he may have received from colleagues.

The lesson here is that getting an introduction to people is simply that—an introduction. That is all. What you do during the call and how you conduct yourself will make the difference as to whether this person will help. Effective presentations require skillful intelligence gathering on your contacts, referrals, target company, and industry. Effective presentations also require a complete game plan of what you want to accomplish during the call.

In the previous chapter, we covered the various fields of the contact list and the difference between a contact and a referral. These are two very important terms for you to understand because they will be used consistently throughout the remainder of the book and you will need to be able to distinguish between the two. As you proceed with your search, you will be constantly adding to your list. You will need to know who everyone is, and what the origin and relevance of their relationship is to you. This is a basic part of the process of building your network of contacts, not just for your next job opportunity, but for your life. This network will always be there to help you, if you manage these relationships properly.

As you go forward, you will be adding contacts who started out as referrals. Referrals who become contacts may become great resources and can provide additional referral names for you. As an example, my nephew Jared was looking for a job in the entertainment business. He called and asked me for help. I was his contact. I gave him a referral, my friend Jeff at NBC. Jeff could not help him, but he gave Jared two other names. Now Jeff became his contact when he called those other people.

Referrals will either get you closer to your next job opportunity, or be the person that actually hires you. You never know where your referral calls will take you.

In this chapter, you will learn how to do your prep work before you pick up the phone to call someone. You will be shown a strategy of how to gather critical information, where to get it, and how to match your skills to your knowledge of the job in order to determine your value to a target company. You need to do some "leg work" in order to come across as credible, manage the call properly, and get people to do what you want them to. As they say in the military, they need the intelligence to make informed decisions. You're going to provide it.

Doing the Due Diligence

Before you actually pick up the phone to call any of your contacts and referrals, you need to look at each and every situation as a unique opportunity. You will need to go through a process that will allow you to come across as the knowledgeable, resourceful, and organized person you are.

Recently I was speaking at a BrassRing's Talent Conference. In three sessions, I addressed more than 750 people. After attending my session, members of my audience were going to walk the trade floor and have an opportunity to speak with some 50 prospective employers. I asked the group, "How many of you have done any due diligence on the companies that you will be meeting with later today?" What do you think the percentage of those who had prepared was? Only 10 percent of the people were informed about their prospective employers. I told the other 90 percent not to go on the floor but to go home, do some homework on their target companies and come back tomorrow. If you are carefully prepared, you will already be among the top 10 percent of all candidates.

The front-end work you do will go a long way towards getting you where you ultimately want to be. You must do whatever you can to gather as much information as possible on the person you are calling and their company.

What should I know?

There are five basic questions you need to answer before you make the phone call:

1. What does this company do and/or what industry are they in?

2. Based on all the research I have done, it appears that this company (or individual, or both possibly) needs help in which areas??

3. Based on what I know about the company, this individual, and my area of expertise, what is my value to this company?

4. Who at this company or industry would recognize my value to the organization (or industry)?

5. What do I really "bring to the party" that is quantifiable, measurable, and makes me stand out from the crowd (both personally and professionally)?

Remember Lucy, the training designer that worked in the financial services field? You were introduced to in Chapter 1. (We used her self-analysis as an example.)

Lucy identified a company for which she wanted to work. She also had a friend working in that company and was preparing to contact her. Before doing so, she needed to answer the same questions you will have to on pages 69-70. Here is how Lucy answered the five basic questions. There is also a short explanation of where this type of information can be found.

1. What does this company do and/or in what industry is it?

The company is a Chicago area federal bank, offering brokerage, lending, and insurance services.

(The answer to this question will either come from your knowledge, or from the research you will be conducting on this company. Research tips appear later in this chapter.)

2. Based on all the research I have done, it appears that this company (or individual, or possibly both) needs help in which areas?

Integrating an online training program into their existing training curriculum.

(The answer to this question will come from the due diligence you will conduct on a particular company. The source(s) of this information will be explained in detail later in this chapter.)

3. Based on what I know about the company, this individual, and my area of expertise, what is my value to this company?

My understanding of adult learning theory and prior experience in developing online training in the financial services industry.

(The answer to this question will come from your responses to the first two questions you completed in your self-analysis.)

4. Who in this company (or in this industry) would realize my value to the organization (or industry)?

The Training Director or Manager of the division.

(The answer to this question will come from your due diligence or from your contact or referral.)

5. What do I really "bring to the party" that is quantifiable, measurable, and makes me stand out from the crowd (both personally and professionally)?

I bring my extensive experience developing online training for the financial services industry and knowledge of adult learning.

(The answer to this question will be a culmination of answers to questions 1 to 4 and the answers you completed in your self-analysis.)

I realize you may not be ready to answer these questions yet. The point is that I want you to see the value of knowing about a company or individual. Here's where to gain this knowledge.

Where do I get this critical information?

There are numerous sources for gathering critical information. Using only one of them may provide you with enough information, however, the more you know, the more of an edge you will have over your competition.

▷ **The people who gave you the referrals.** These contacts may be able to tell you a lot about the people you are calling. From conversations with your contacts, you can learn how the referrals are personally and professionally, and what their family situations, interests, and hobbies are. You may also gain some insight into what is going on in the company, and what your target audience's "hot buttons" are. This way you can really have meaningful conversations and capitalize on the relationships that exist between your contacts and referrals. Remember the story about Nick and Victoria? It's clear that the time I spent with Victoria and the probing questions she asked about the hiring manger really paid off. Also, she asked me to call ahead on her behalf, which I did. Don't be afraid to ask your contact to make that initial call for you, too. The worst thing they can say is no.

▷ **People you know that are currently working or have previously worked for or with the company.** These people will be able to give you tremendous insight into the company. This information should allow you to ask some great questions of the referral or contact. The type of insights you can get from insiders might be: how the company is doing, how the company is viewed in its industry and by their competition, what makes this a good company to work for, or the company's culture and environment.

The types of questions you ask and answers you give your insider contact will send a strong message back to your contact or referral that says "This person has done their homework."

▷ **People you know who are currently working, or have previously worked with your contact or referral.** If you can find someone who knows the person that you're about to call very well, it's invaluable. Gathering information about your contacts or referrals from someone who has actually spent 40-plus hours per week with them will provide you with invaluable information on many levels. It will certainly help you manage the conversation and give you a real competitive advantage. Back to that situation with Victoria, who was trying to get a recruiting position with the office supply retailer. Besides speaking with me, Victoria remembered that someone she knew (Dennis) used to work for the Hiring Manager. Even though Dennis did not leave the company on the best of terms, she called him. She learned about the hiring manager's style, disposition, and expectations.

When Victoria goes in for her interviews, she will have gained more insight into the company, department, and individual than probably any other candidate.

> **The Internet.** Technology has allowed us to gather a tremendous amount of information in the public domain. Just because you developed significant information from the people mentioned above, it is important that you get the big picture, too. In searching on the Internet for either individuals or companies, there are a few search engines worth mentioning to access information, they are:

- *Google.com*

- *Yahoo.com*

- *Hoovers.com*

- *Ask Jeeves.com*

- *AltaVista.com*

- *AOL.com*

- *MSN.com*

- *Search.com*

- *Bloomberg.com*

> **The company Website.** The information you gain from this source is invaluable. You must always check a company Website as part of your due diligence regardless of the amount of other information you have accessed. This is the place you gain real insight to what the company wants you to know about them. Here is where you should look and what you should look for on a company Website:

➤ *Home Page* or *About Us*. This is the place to get a great overview about who the company is, what it does, and who its clients are.

➤ *Products and Services* or *Capabilities*. This will give you insight into what types of products and services they offer.

➤ *Investor Relations*. If the company is public, you can look at its financial reports to view the size of the company, and more importantly, how well it is doing.

➤ *Media* or *Press*. It is particularly important that you cover this section. This will provide you with current happenings within an organization, such as new product release, acquisitions, recognition in its industry, or changes in senior management. You want to acknowledge and discuss this information when you have a conversation with your contact or referrals, demonstrating you have done your homework and you are up to speed as to what is happening with the company that you want to join.

➤ *Management Team*. When looking at the management team, you might recognize a name of someone you know who could become a contact, referral, or just some one that can help you in the process. Look at everyone to see if you can locate some type of connection. You can ask your network of contacts what they might know about a member of the senior management team. More often than you guess, you will find that someone you know went to the same college, or perhaps worked at a company where your contact used to work. If you look hard enough, you will find a connection that can help.

Last year I was a speaker at the Quinnipiac Chamber of Commerce. I met someone from a regional bank that expressed interest in working with me. When I got back to the office, I went onto their Website. When I looked at the management team, I recognized the Executive Vice President and thought he was someone I had played golf with in a Pro-Am tournament many years ago. When I got home, I went through my paperwork and found a picture from that day. I called him the next day and told him about the conversation I had with someone else from his bank at the Chamber function. He offered his help and asked me to keep him apprised of my progress. That bank is now a client. The fact is: You simply do not know where the connection is going to be made when building your *SuperNetwork*.

> **Competitors.** Go to their Websites, too. See what the "other guy" is doing and how they represent themselves in the marketplace. Try to understand how your contacts or referrals differentiate themselves from their competition. You want to demonstrate that you are ready to be part of a team and that you are a strategic thinker. Perhaps you want to pick something out to discuss and ask the contact or referral about the competition. This again is a great way to demonstrate to your target audience that you are different from 95 percent of the people that go after finding a new job with minimal effort on the front end. Your contact or referral will appreciate the way you are approaching this search.

Another reason why you want to look at the competition is because these companies may, at some time, be of interest to you if things do not come to fruition with the company you originally targeted. This way, the investment you will have made in your prescribed industry of interest will potentially have an alternative payoff. Your time will not be for naught. As an example, Jacqueline, an experienced software sales executive from Siebel, wants to sell for Oracle. Oracle's biggest competitors are PeopleSoft and SAP, and she did her homework on all three companies. If things do not work out for her at Oracle, do you think the PeopleSoft or SAP may have a need for her services? Possibly. Based on her experience and initial due diligence she should pursue them also, further utilizing the time she has already invested.

➤ **User Groups.** Birds of a feather do flock together. People that are members of user groups pride themselves on having what I refer to as "course knowledge." That's a golf term for knowing the terrain (in this case of their business), what obstacles to avoid, how to avoid them, and what you need to do to be successful. The internal fabric of groups with this course knowledge is called "knowledge transfer." If possible, access groups like this also. Again, their insight into a company or individual may be invaluable. Just remember why you are asking for their help in the first place—it's to gather information on an individual or company.

➤ **Trade associations.** These are very similar to user groups. Most professionals belong to some group. They use their membership to stay current on what's happening in the field, but they use it as a networking forum, too. Not only do members of a trade association often share intimate knowledge about a company or individual, but they can also become referrals or contacts for you to open up other doors into additional companies. If you are a member of any of these types of organizations, try to get the membership directory. Make sure you are judicious when using it. Remember: You want to be very focused in your approach. Just because you get a list like this does not mean you should call everyone.

What happens if I don't know anyone in the company and have tried everything and have still come up dry?

Yes, of course that is a possibility. My advice is to think outside the box, challenge yourself, and not accept defeat. Put yourself into a mindset that there must be someone that can get you this information. Push yourself past where others would have given up. I encourage you to push a little harder—you just may open up a door you never imagined. This challenge was raised in one of my workshops. I hope it will get you to think outside the box if you are confronted with what appears to be a dead end.

Anne Marie, a purchasing manager, was downsized and was looking for another opportunity. She identified a bell manufacturing company that interested her and was located near Waterbury, Connecticut. This company had been around for 30 years and was privately held. They did not have a Website, and after exhausting her network of contacts, she could not identify anyone she knew who could help her access company information or get in the door. She was very frustrated. I probed a little to see if we could find a few ways that she had not thought of that may allow her to "go against the grain."

Here are the options we developed:

> ➤ Call the company to inquire if they have a brochure and have one sent.

➤ Check the Thomas Registry of Manufacturers to see if they are listed and perhaps get the names and titles of the management team. If Anne Marie were to get the names, she could then work back through her SuperNetwork to see if anyone recognizes a name.

➤ Contact the Waterbury Chamber of Commerce to see if the company is a member. More than likely, someone from the Chamber will know the principals of the bell manufacturer.

As we discussed these new options, Anne Marie realized she had more avenues through which to pursue this opportunity. She was pretty sure that, between her contacts and other people that worked and lived in the Waterbury area, someone would be able to help her in her quest. She then decided that using her contacts to go through the Chamber of Commerce made the most sense.

The point is that even if you don't know anyone in the company, if you put together a strategy, you'll be amazed what you can come up with. In Chapter 6, you will be introduced to the concept of having a mentor help you through your job search process. Thes type of brainstorming session I did with Anne Marie is the kind of thing you may want to go through with your mentor. You may not have all the answers and you are not expected to. However, if you put in the effort, the results will follow.

Dead in the Water!

I can't possibly overstate it enough that you can't just "wing it" when you call someone. Getting people to do what you want them to do is a reflection of how well you manage a phone call.

You might be having what you think is a successful phone call but inevitably your contact or referral is going to ask one of these questions:

➤ What do you know about our company?

➤ What do you know about our industry?

➤ Do you understand what we do here?

If you say, "I do not know that much," or try to bluff your way through, in all likelihood, you will have destroyed your chances of success with the call and with this contact in particular. You will lose all credibility with this person. More importantly, you probably will have "burned" this contact not just for this opportunity, but for future ones. In addition, when your name comes up in future conversations, this person will be unlikely to volunteer positive thoughts about you. As I mentioned previously, you never know which contact will be the one to steer you toward your ultimate goal. You can not afford to blow it by being unprepared.

The way to ensure this won't happen to you is by doing your due diligence—the necessary, up front work that has been described previously in this chapter. Besides being properly prepared for every conversation you have with people, this knowledge will give you confidence and a real competitive advantage.

By doing this work and impressing your target audience, you will be making it very easy for them to assist you now and in the future. Remember the story about Nick from the beginning of this chapter? I had spoken with Jim, the vice president of taxes, subsequent to Nick's conversation. I asked, "Suppose Nick had demonstrated to you that he had done some homework on your company, and Nick knew your firm had just made an acquisition and recently became the largest in your field, and his background was in Fund Administration, would you have taken Nick's resume to the Vice President of Fund Administration because he may be a good fit?" Jim said he would have. When I asked why he said, "Because if Nick would have told me what he was looking for, that he had an idea where he might have fit in the organization, and if he knew a little bit about the company, in particular about the acquisition which was written up in all the major newspapers, he would have made it easy for me to help. But Nick did none of that, and I was not about to go out of my way for him, even though Steve asked me as a favor to speak with him. I did that, but that was it."

Because Nick was directionless, Jim was not motivated or willing to take the time to get Nick on track, or go out of his way to help him. This was a networking disaster. Don't be like Nick. Do the necessary work, and you will leave a favorable impression with people when you call them.

Once you have done the necessary due diligence, you should be able to complete these preparation questions (page 79-81) for each person and company you contact. You will carry the answers forward in Chapter 4 when you are preparing your call strategy and objective, and again in Chapter 5 when you are preparing your phone script. Choose a company you are interested in and complete the following questions:

1.   What does this company do and/or in what industry is it? *(This will come from your due diligence.)*

_____

_____

_____

2. **Based on all the research I have done it appears that this company (or individual, or both possibly) needs help in which areas?**
(This will also come from your due diligence.)

_____

_____

_____

_____

_____

3. **Based on what I know about the company, this individual, and my area of expertise, what is my value to this company?**
(This should be a combination of your due diligence and your self-analysis answers.)

_____

_____

_____

_____

_____

_____

_____

4. Who at this company (or in this industry) would realize my value to the organization (or in this industry)?
(This will come from your due diligence)

_____

_____

_____

_____

_____

5. What do I really "bring to the party" that is quantifiable, measurable, and makes me stand out from the crowd (both personally and professionally)?
(This should be a combination of your due diligence and self-analysis answers)

_____

_____

_____

_____

_____

_____

Pop Quiz

This chapter has focused on showing you the value of proper preparation, how and where to get that knowledge, the importance of making a favorable impression by gathering as much information as possible, the danger of not being prepared for the initial conversation, and the importance of being able to discern and articulate your value to a given company.

1. What percentage of people do the necessary due diligence before they speak to prospective companies?

    a. 10 percent.

    b. 30 percent.

    c. 50 percent.

    d. 80 percent.

2. Where are the best sources of information you can get on a person or company?

    a. The newspaper.

    b. A variety of sources including he Internet, company Websites, referrals, competitors, and Google.

    c. Myself, friends, and neighbors.

3. "Dead in the water" means?

    a. Fish died.

    b. Man over board.

    c. I was trying to "wing it" when I made a call and was stopped in my tracks when I was asked, "What do you know about our company?"

If you answered 1a, 2b, and 3c (you better have gotten that one), you really are paying attention and are ready now to apply what you have learned so far and proceed to Chapter 4.

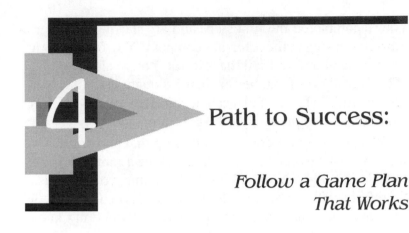

Path to Success:

Follow a Game Plan That Works

Chuck hung up the phone and swung around his swivel chair as his wife entered the room with a mug of coffee. "How are the networking calls going, honey?" she asked.

"Great! I just called Roy Jones at ICI. He told me that Tom Norman was hiring for the new team they're putting together—and Tom was the guy who sat next to me at dinner at the conference last month. I remember he told me that he used to work for Carol Swenson. Carol knows that I have the perfect background to manage that team! I'm going to call her and ask her to call him about me. I'll ask her to tell him about the project I did for her last year—that will give me some credibility, and he'll be waiting for my call."

You've called your contacts and they have given you the names of some people to call. This is getting exciting, isn't it?

You've completed the first steps and are starting to picture yourself working at the referral's company. You feel ready to pick up the phone and call the referral. You're also thinking, "This is really working, better than I thought it would! Networking isn't so hard—I just call people, they give me names, I follow up—and pretty soon I'll get a great job."

Well, stop right there—don't pick up that phone yet! Using networking to get names without having a game plan is an exercise in futility. You will just be "spinning your wheels." No referral will be able to help if you can't articulate exactly what you want that person to do for you. If you don't know where you're going, no road will be able to get you there. That's why you have to make a plan.

If you do everything prescribed in this chapter, you will get where you want to be, and you will find your next job in far less time than it will take the rest of your competition (who *think* that they know how to network). Do you know what they have going for them? They just have a list of contacts. That's all. What they don't have is a plan.

Before you pick up the phone, you need to be prepared. You can't just "wing it," rely on your instincts, and hope for the best. A good referral is pure gold—and one of your referrals is likely to be the person who opens the door to a job that will change your life. Your first contact with your referrals are critical to getting your next job, and the objective of this chapter is to put you in the best possible position to get the response you want every time you call.

This chapter will also give you a plan and all the tools you need to make a big impression on each referral, and to motivate that person to help you. You are going to make it so easy for that person to help you that it will not feel like an inconvenience or a hardship. You will be able to articulate and demonstrate your value proposition so well that the referral will feel very comfortable helping you.

The Value of a Warm Call

Have you ever heard the expression, "It's not what you know, but who you know?" That saying is absolutely true. Your referrals can open doors that you simply could not open on your own. Although a cold call to a stranger will hardly ever get you anywhere, a warm call that is based on a referral will greatly increase your chances of being heard. What do you think would happen if you tried to cold call Bill Gates? Do you think you'd even get through to him? But what if you called his office and said that Paul Allen—Bill's former partner and good friend—was a friend of yours and suggested that you call him. Do you think that your chances of reaching Bill Gates would improve? Using the names of your contacts properly will open doors to people who wouldn't speak to you otherwise.

An even more effective way to get a referral's attention is to ask your contact to call first to introduce you. This will set the stage so that the referral will be expecting your call. Your contact will be most likely to do this if the two of you have a particularly strong relationship, or if your contact has a lot of respect for your abilities. Although persuading your contact to make an introductory call may not always be possible, it's certainly worth asking about. Make it your standard procedure to always ask your contact to call the referral first. What's the worst that can happen? Paul Allen might say no. But you can still call the referral and use your contact's name to break the ice. Either way, a warm call greatly increases the chances that you will be successful.

Peel the Onion

Networking to find the person who can really help you is similar to peeling an onion. Usually you will have to go through many layers before you get to the core (the person you really need to talk to). Reaching this person may require repeated phone calls—there may be four, five, or even six degrees of separation between your initial contact and the person to whom you really need to talk. You must keep calling because you simply never know from where your next opportunity will come. You have to follow up and follow through on every lead you receive. It may take one phone call, or it may take far more than that. Accept the reality that this process may take substantial effort before it pays the ultimate dividend.

On average, each person you call will refer you to at least two more people. Although some contacts may not give you any referrals, others will give you many. This means that by calling each of the 80 contacts on your A, B, C, and D contact lists (see Chapter 2) you should end up with 160 referrals—for a starting network of 240 people. If you develop and maintain this list effectively, it will continue to grow, and more people will be helping you find your next opportunity.

Learn to Name Drop Properly

A warm call involves using your contact's name to get the referral's attention. Although name dropping can open the door for you, you need to manage it properly. To do so, you need to understand the relationship between the contact and referral. Your ability to use the contact's name appropriately will go a long way toward establishing your credibility with the referral. Your introduction to a referral who is a close personal friend of your contact will be significantly different than your introduction to a referral who is just a casual business acquaintance of your contact.

Although your contact's name can open the door for you, be careful not to mention too many other names. How many times have you heard someone say, "He's such a name dropper!"? Most people consider name-dropping to be unattractive and pretentious. If you "drop" too many names, your referral may start to think that you're arrogant, or too well connected to need help. If you mention the names of any other people to your referral, make sure that those names are relevant to the conversation, and that you mention them in the proper context and at an appropriate time. They arise naturally out of the flow of the conversation, rather than coming out of nowhere. There's a big difference between advertising the names of all your important friends and conversing naturally about your shared experiences and acquaintances.

While playing golf recently, my friend Mark was teamed with Jeff, who introduced himself as a TV comedy writer from California. Mark asked Jeff if he knew his friend Lee Kaye, who manages comedy writers. Jeff said that although he didn't know Lee personally, he knew of him. Later in the round, Jeff mentioned that he enjoyed shopping for clothes with his wife—and Mark asked if he had ever shopped at Fred Siegal in Santa Monica. Jeff said that it was his favorite store, and added, "Man, you really get around." Jeff had a positive impression of Mark, because Mark's remarks grew naturally out of their conversation.

Create Your Own Action Plan

Now that we've covered some key points, it's time to learn how to create your action plan and fine tune it to make every step clear. Here are the key ingredients that we will cover in the rest of this chapter:

➤ **Be credible.** Your referral won't make a strong effort on your behalf unless you know how to develop and maintain your credibility.

➤ **Plan your strategy.** To be successful, you'll need a strategy and a plan—a road map to help you reach your objective.

➤ **Set your call objectives.** You need to have a clear, specific, and measurable objective for each call. Each objective will automatically lead you to another action step.

➤ **Prepare for the call.** You'll need to do prep work, or due diligence, that will demonstrate your unique approach and the distinctive value that you have to offer each contact.

➤ **Follow the essential do's and don'ts.** You'll need to know the key things to do and say—and what not to do and say—in order to make a good impression.

➤ **Do a post-call debriefing.** To assess your progress, you'll need to promptly determine whether each call was successful.

➤ **Follow up and follow through.** After making a call, you will need to know how to follow up on it to continue moving toward your goal.

Be Credible

When you call your referral, you must come across as credible. There are three factors that you can use to establish your credibility:

1. Establishing good reputation for yourself in advance.

2. Associating yourself with someone who already has credibility—your contact.

3. Earning credibility by how you conduct yourself during the initial call.

A good reputation

Although it's often true that "your reputation precedes you," this can be either a blessing or a curse. It's important to try to honestly assess how you are viewed by others. If your reputation is positive, the beginning of the conversation probably will go well. However, at this stage, your previous reputation will have only a temporary effect—even the best reputation may be nullified if you don't make a good impression during the phone call.

Credibility by association

By contacting a referral on the strength of someone else's reputation, you gain an opening to have your voice heard. The stronger the link between the contact and the referral, the better that opportunity will be. Ideally, your contact will call the referral first to set the stage for your call, but that's not always possible. And, as with a good reputation, the effect of credibility by association is only temporary. To create a lasting positive impression, you must carry yourself well and be able to clearly articulate your message.

Earning credibility through your conduct

Earning credibility through your conduct is the only way to gain lasting credibility. You must begin to earn it from the start of the first phone call, by being articulate, clear, concise, professional, and courteous. A positive impression here will set the tone of your entire relationship with this contact, and allow you to fully leverage the potential of this networking opportunity. Demonstrating your networking skills is a selling point in itself, because people will assume that this is a reflection of your overall competence.

One key factor in gaining credibility is to demonstrate your understanding of the referral's company, industry, accomplishments, and interests. It is also essential that you be able to clearly articulate the valueable skills that you will bring to the organization. Finally, your ability to confidently request what you would like the contact to do on your behalf will demonstrate that you are focused and in control.

Now that you understand the importance of earning credibility, and some of the ways to establish it, it's time to move to the next phase—planning your strategy.

Plan Your Strategy

You already know what type of job you want (based on the exercise you did in Chapter 1). Now you need to put together a plan. There are six steps involved in planning your strategy:

1. Evaluate your current position.

2. Evaluate the alternatives.

3. Choose the best option.

4. Identify target companies or organizations.

5. Research target companies or organizations.

6. Implement the strategy you have chosen.

Write down your answers to these six steps on the summary form at the end of this chapter. Here's an example to show how you might proceed.

1. **Evaluate your current position:** You are a salesperson, and for the last four years you have worked for a national telecommunications company selling to financial service companies in Massachusetts, where you live. However, the market has gone soft, and you have just been laid off.

2. **Evaluate your alternatives:** Because of the downturn in the industry, you feel it is unlikely that you will be able to find a local position in the telecom industry. However, your skills may be transferable to other local high-tech companies or to other local companies. You realize that your telecom experience could be useful to companies that sell to the financial services industry. You could also consider other parts of the country where the telecom industry is still thriving. Because you have large company experience, you might consider other large national organizations. Finally, for strategic purposes, you might consider taking a temporary job while you look for a full-time position.

3. **Choose the best option:** You decide that you want to stay in Massachusetts and parlay your sales skills in other areas of the high-tech sector, or to emerging industries, such as security software, e-commerce software, or professional service companies that sell to the financial services industry.

4. **Identify target companies or organizations:** You research to identify the top 10 companies in your area that could use your skills and that might be places where you'd like to work. You have now identified your target companies.

5. **Research target companies thoroughly:** You thoroughly research each target company, identifying which division you want to work in, what your title would be in that organization, how that division creates value, and how you would create value for that specific group. You then try to find out who heads that division, who you would be reporting to, and who is hiring for that division.

6. **Implement your strategy:** You have begun forming your strategy. You have evaluated all your options, you have identified and researched your target companies, and you have a goal in mind. You are ready to take the next step and set your call objectives.

Set Your Call Objectives

It's very important to have an end result clear in your mind before you make each call. Remember: You want to make it easy for people to help you. Before you call any referral, you must ask yourself the following questions:

➤ What do I want to accomplish in this phone call?

➤ What do I want this person to do on my behalf?

Write the answers to these questions down on the summary form at the end of this chapter (page 103-105), and keep them in front of you when you make the call. You don't want to have a nice conversation, and suddenly realize, after you hung up, that you didn't accomplish your initial objectives.

Here are some samples of call objectives:

- ➤ Schedule a face-to-face meeting.
- ➤ Send your resume to this person.
- ➤ Find out if there are any job opportunities in this person's company.
- ➤ If this is not the right person, get an introduction to other people in this company.
- ➤ Have this person send your resume to other people.
- ➤ Ask for another referral.
- ➤ Ask to schedule a meeting with someone this person knows on your behalf.
- ➤ Arrange a future callback to exchange ideas.
- ➤ Arrange a callback at a specific future date to find out if the situation has changed.

Your call objectives need to be well thought out, clearly defined, and narrow enough that the desired result will be achievable. Reaching each objective should trigger another event or action that should also be as specific as possible, to maximize this contact's ability to assist you. For example, let's say that you have found a contact who is willing to sponsor you within their company. Don't just send that person your resume without direction; this will leave you wondering exactly where it went and who saw it. Instead, find out, as specifically as possible, what the sponsor will be doing with it.

Now that you have prepared your call objectives, you need to do the research that will ensure that you make a good impression during the phone call.

Prepare For the Call

Before you actually pick up the phone, you need to review the situation that with which you are faced with and do some research on it. Your ability to get the other person to do what you want will generally be determined by the impression that you make in the first phone call. To make a good impression, you must come across as knowledgeable, resourceful, and organized. This means that you need to gather as much information as you can about both the person and the company that you are calling, as previously described. (See Chapter 3 for a more thorough explanation of how and where to gather information from different sources.)

If the referral asks you what you know about their company, and you can't make any substantive comments, you will have damaged both your credibility and your chances for success with this contact. Demonstrating that you have done some thorough research up front will also distinguish you from your competition.

After you have done all that research, you might think that you're finally ready to pick up the phone. However, before you call, it's important to sit down and carefully answer the following questions based on your research (you can use the summary form at the end of the chapter):

➤ What does this company do and what industry is it in?

➤ What do I know about this referral and company? How can I use that information in the call?

➤ Based on my research, it appears that this company or person may need help in what areas?

➤ What value can I offer this person, company, or industry that is quantifiable, measurable, and makes me stand out from the crowd?

➤ Who in this company would understand my value to the organization?

In addition to completing these questions, you need to do a few more things before you make the phone call. Take out the Self-Analysis form that you filled out in Chapter 1, as well as the call objectives and strategy that you prepared for this referral. Keep this information with you when you make the phone call.

You have put a lot of time and effort into your preparation, and you will only have one chance to make a favorable first impression. Before you pick up that phone, you need to be sure that you are observing some essential do's and don'ts.

Follow Essential Do's and Don'ts

There are some key things that you need to remember to do in every call. There are also key things that you should never do—because one bad statement can be more powerful than 10 good recommendations. To make a good impression, be sure to observe the following guidelines for every call:

Essential do's

✓ **Remember, it's just a phone.** If you feel intimidated, the phone will feel like a 20-pound barbell. But if your confidence level is high, it will feel as light as a feather.

✓ **Call with a positive attitude.** People can sense your mood over the phone. If you're feeling discouraged, depressed, worried, or desperate, it will come across over the phone. Call only when you're feeling positive and upbeat.

✓ **Carry yourself like a winner.** Although Michael Jordan may not win every game, he always carries himself like a winner. His swagger and tone of voice tell people that, win or lose, this guy is a champion. You need to carry yourself in the same manner.

✓ **Speak with confidence.** Let the person you're calling feel your energy, passion, and interest. Show some energy and excitement, without going overboard.

✓ **Use inflections.** Make your points with vocal variety and emphasis. Don't speak in a monotone. If you aren't sure of how your voice sounds, use a tape recorder to find out.

✓ **Call from a quiet area.** If you're calling from work, go to an office where you can close the door and have some privacy. If you're calling from home, go to a room where no one will enter or bother you. You don't want the referral to hear TV, radio, or family noise in the background.

✓ **Keep a glass of water nearby.** If you become engaged in a long conversation, your throat may get dry. Have a glass of water nearby so that you can remain focused on the phone call.

✓ **Have a pad and two pens handy.** You need to be prepared to take notes without interrupting the flow of the conversation.

✓ **Ask for action.** Former Speaker of the House Tip O'Neill always said, "People like to be asked, and people like to be thanked." He learned that lesson the hard way—he lost his first election because he didn't ask people for their votes. You can't afford to make the same mistake. You must ask for your referral's help and then hold that person accountable for the commitments that have been made. Don't hesitate to call back a few times to make sure that they fulfill those commitments.

✓ **Always end the conversation on a positive note.** Make sure that the referral leaves the conversation feeling good about helping you.

Essential don'ts

✗ **Don't call unprepared.** Know your audience before you call. Make sure that you have done all your due diligence, as previously described.

✗ **Don't call from a cell phone.** Always call from a landline. Even the best cell phones are not as good as conventional phones—they all have dead areas, and you don't want to be cut off in mid-sentence. Also, using a landline demonstrates that you are giving this important phone call with the respect and privacy that it deserves. Interference on the phone line can break your rhythm and distract the other person from your message.

✗ **Don't call while driving.** You simply can't give the other person your complete attention and concentration while driving. It's impossible to talk on the phone, read your notes, and drive at the same time. Also, it's an accident waiting to happen.

✗ **Don't inflate your background or abilities.** You are who you are—be comfortable with it. If the referral senses that you aren't being honest, your credibility will be shot, and the phone call will be over.

✗ **Don't fail to listen.** Pay attention to what your referral is saying. People can sense if you aren't listening to them. It's rude, and it makes a bad impression. It will also impede your ability to respond effectively during the conversation.

✗ **Don't interrupt.** Keep in mind that you are asking this person to help you. If you repeatedly cut the referral off in mid-sentence, you will make a bad impression and are unlikely to get the help that you are seeking. If there's a point that you don't want to forget, write it down and bring it up when there is a break in the conversation.

✗ **Don't fail to speak up.** If you provide too little information, the referral may think that you lack depth, drive, or intelligence. To make a favorable impression, you must demonstrate that you are well informed, thorough, and capable. You can't do that if you don't say anything.

✗ **Don't share too much information.** You don't need to tell the referral your life story or all the details of what happened on your last job. Before you call, you will set a strategy and an objective. Do not stray from that purpose. Also, remember that your referral's time is valuable.

✗ **Don't "bad-mouth" other people or companies.** Negative talk is counterproductive, it detracts from your message, and it makes you look weak, no matter how justified it is. Also, your referral may have friends in the other company, or may think he or she knows more than you do about the person you are discussing.

✗ Don't be afraid to ask tough questions. Asking tough questions will get you closer to your goal and will help you figure out whether this person will be able to help you. Capable people will respect you for asking the questions that others would avoid. For example, let's say that your due diligence shows that this company hasn't been profitable lately. You might ask, "My research indicates that you've had three losing quarters in a row. I was wondering what measures the company has been taking to turn this around?" By asking this, you will not only get the answer you need to properly evaluate the company, you will also differentiate yourself from other candidates who don't have the confidence to ask such a tough question. This kind of question can also lead to an opportunity to ask a question that suggests your value to the organization, such as, "Does this mean that you are even more actively looking for people who can make a direct contribution to the bottom line?"

✗ Don't apologize for asking for help. When you're networking to find a job, it's perfectly acceptable to ask for help, so don't apologize for doing so. As long as you maintain a polite, professional, confident manner, most people will respect your requests. Remember that networking is a two-way street, and, someday, you may be in a position to return the favor.

✗ **Don't let your referral "off the hook."** There's nothing wrong with polite, professional persistence. If you need to, call back a few times in order to get your referral to do what they said they would do. Don't be shy, even if you are. Remember: This is your career and your life—it's too important to not give it your all.

Do a Post-Call Debriefing

After you finish each phone conversation, you need to take a moment to figure out whether it was successful and what you have accomplished. Immediately after the call, ask yourself the following questions:

➤ Did I reach my goal for the call?

➤ Did I accomplish my call objective?

It's up to you to set expectations of what you are trying to achieve. Your objectives need to be clearly defined and narrowly focused, so that when you finish each phone call, you'll know right away whether you have reached your call objective. Consistently achieving your short-term objectives will quickly move you forward toward your ultimate goal—finding your next job.

Follow Up and Follow Through

The way that you follow up and follow through after each call is extremely important. Most conversations with a contact will trigger some type of action on your part. You may have been asked to send a resume or to follow up with email. Because actions speak louder than words, always do what you say you are going to do in a timely manner.

Here are some scenarios that are likely to occur and how you should follow up on them:

The referral asked you to send your resume.

Find out when the referral wants the resume and how they would like to receive it (e-mail, fax, regular mail). Check that all the contact information on your resume is accurate, and then send it out expeditiously.

The referral gave you the names of some other people to call.

Be sure that you understand exactly how the referral would like to handle this. Will the referral be calling ahead to introduce you, or are you supposed to call and mention the referral's name? Either way, make a note in your planner to call the new people on the day that you agreed to do it.

The referral is scheduling a meeting or an interview for you.

Agree on a date and time during the call, and immediately record it in your planner.

As you follow up, you need to remain organized or learn to prioritize your activities. You must always live up to your commitments. Stay focused, and don't let anything or anyone get in the way of what you need to do. Remember that your referrals will be judging you by how you follow up and conduct yourself.

Don't get busy with new activities but let existing commitments slide, ignoring the negative impression that this will make on other people. Your credibility is on the line here, and you must execute effectively. Mrs. Fields (the cookie mogul) says, "Good enough never is." Don't just meet expectations— exceed them.

Follow through by staying in touch or to showing your appreciation to your contacts and referrals. Here a few suggestions for staying in touch:

➤ **Phone calls.** Keep your contact in the loop as your job search progresses, especially about any developments with the people to whom he or she introduced you.

➤ **E-mail.** Same as the follow up phone call. Keep all e-mails short and simple.

➤ **Send an article.** If you know that your contact has interests in certain subjects, and you see an interesting article on such topics, send it along. It shows that you are thinking about him or her.

➤ **Offer your help.** Offer to reciprocate by asking if there is anything that you can do for your contact. For example, maybe your contact is planning to buy a car, and you have a contact at a dealership. Maybe you can offer some help painting a room in his or her house. Give and take will take you a long way.

➤ **Become a referral.** Perhaps you can introduce your contact to someone who can help. Now you are becoming a resource for others.

➤ **Personal updates.** Let people know what's happening in your personal life—for example, graduations, or weddings. This humanizes you and lets people see you in a different light.

➤ **Invitations.** Invite a contact to a ball game, movie, or dinner. It's another way of saying thank you and gives you a chance to spend some time with him or her.

➤ **Recreational activities.** Invite your contact to go fishing, play golf, or go for a run.

➤ **Send holiday cards.** In addition to the traditional holidays, you can stand out from the crowd by sending a card on the occasion of another holiday—include a warm note, a thank you, or a personal update.

CHAPTER 4 SUMMARY FORM

Call Strategy

My current position is:

_____

_____

My alternatives are:

_____

_____

_____

The option I choose is:

_____

_____

Call Objectives

What do I want this person to do for me?

_____

_____

What do I want to accomplish in this call?

_____

_____

Call Prep Questions

What does this company do/what industry are they in?

_____

_____

What do I know and how can I use it during this call?

_____

_____

_____

_____

_____

_____

In what does this company or individual appears to need help?

_____

_____

_____

_____

The quantifiable, measurable, and distinctive value that I offer is:

_____

_____

_____

_____

_____

_____

Who in this company or industry would realize my value?

_____

_____

_____

Are You Ready to Get on the Phone?

Yes No

☐ ☐ 1. Do you know what it means to "peel the onion?"

☐ ☐ 2. Have you done your due diligence?

☐ ☐ 3. Do you have a call strategy?

☐ ☐ 4. Do you know what your call objective is?

☐ ☐ 5. Do you have the reference material on the Referral (either person, company, or industry)?

☐ ☐ 6. Do you have your profile completed?

☐ ☐ 7. Are you prepared to ask the tough questions, and "not let people off the hook?"

☐ ☐ 8. Do you know what to avoid doing?

☐ ☐ 9. Are you prepared to have a call debriefing to determine whether your call was successful?

☐ ☐ 10. Do you understand the importance of timely follow up and follow through?

If you can answer yes to all these questions, you are ready to prepare your phone script. If you answered no to any of these questions, take a few minutes to reread the part(s) you may have missed. Remember you are building your SuperNetwork link by link. In order to have a solid foundation, you must follow the directions.

Prize-winning Scripts:

Develop an Effective Pitch

Diane wanted that senior radiographer position at the children's hospital—it was her professional passion. Human Resources told her that she had to talk to Dr. Hartley first, whose schedule was extremely tight, and that it might take weeks to get an appointment with her. Dianne was determined. This job was perfect for her. She sat down and carefully crafted what to say to get Dr. Hartley's attention. It worked! Diane left the message for her and Dr. Hartley called back the same day. The first interview was set for the following Wednesday.

At this time, you have completed the necessary preparation to make a successful call resulting in increasing your network of contacts and bringing you closer to your goal of finding your next job opportunity in less time. You have figured out what you want to, where you want to do it, and whom you want to call. You have a successful strategy, know your call objective, have done your due diligence, and are finally ready to get on the phone. If you can agree with these statements, you are ready!

Because you are about to get on the phone and ask for a favor, you need a good sales pitch. Every effective sales pitch has certain elements designed to steer the conversation in a way that ensures the outcome you desire. What you say, how you say it, and the easier you make it for people to help will go a long way in determining how successful your conversation will be.

There is no better time than the present to start reaching out to your network of contacts. What you are going to learn in this chapter is how to develop an effective script. You will be shown several time-tested sample scripts, which you can tailor to fit your own personality. These sample scripts are much more of a guideline than an absolute rule. You need to blend these samples into your own style when creating your script. You must feel comfortable with whatever comes out of your mouth. People can sense when you are reading a canned speech. (Can't you hear it when the telemarketers call your house? You just want to hang up just because you can tell they're reading. Don't let this happen to you).

Lucy, the training developer, will re-emerge in this chapter. You will review her sample script and also a transcript of a real-life call she made. Tailor the sample scripts to create a few that you feel comfortable with, and be yourself.

This chapter will provide you with the elements of an effective script when speaking with contacts and referrals, covering:

→ What to say.

→ How to ask for help.

➤ Articulating a clear understanding to the contact of why you are calling.

➤ Articulating a clear understanding of what you want them to do for you.

➤ Utilizing information gathered from your self-analysis, due diligence, strategy, and call objective.

➤ If appropriate, asking the contact to provide you with the name of the "right" person you should contact next.

As defined earlier, a contact and a referral are two different people. The way you approach them must be different also. You will also learn how to hold them accountable, ensuring that your phone call will result in moving this process forward.

How will you know whether your phone call was successful? You'll know by conducting the call debriefing that was outlined in the previous chapter. You will be shown how to measure the success of your phone calls by reviewing a quick check list that will indicate whether you were as effective as you thought you were.

Let's start by putting together a script when you're making a call to a contact. Your initial call should:

➤ **Be focused and specific.** Use the information from your self-analysis.

➤ **Have a stated reason for the call.** What do you want to do professionally (which should be taken from completed self-analysis)? What do you want this contact to do for you?

➤ **Be succinct and clear.** You must give people a road map so they can help you. If you are vague or lack clarity, the likelihood of succeeding will decrease. Just ask Nick from Chapter 3. If you can clearly articulate your interest in a concise manner, people are more likely to start thinking of others they know in their field or similar companies and individuals they can recommend contacting.

Phone Call Script

You need to give your contact an idea of what type of company or industry you are looking for. If the situation dictates, you might even mention the specific company. You may ask them if they know a particular person, or the "right" person to contact at a specific company. The key here is not to look for just any name, but to find the "right" person.

1. **Setting the stage.** Start the conversation by exchanging pleasantries—make sure you ask about them. Slow yourself down. You don't want to come across as desperate or as only being interested in having them help you. After you get through the pleasantries you may want to say:

    "I was recently laid off and could really use your help."

    "I need your help. I have made a decision to leave my company."

    "I could really use your help."

    "I am no longer at Company XYZ and I'd like to ask you for your help."

"My company just went through a downsizing, and my position was eliminated. I could really use your help."

2. **Valuing their time.** Make sure you have their undivided attention. Always ask if this is a good time to speak with them. You want to make sure your contact is paying attention and appreciates that this is very important to you. If there are any distractions, you won't get the undivided attention you need to get the most out of this contact. Most callers fail to ask the important following question and just leap ahead into their speech. Don't let this happen to you. At this point, you want to say:

"Do you have some time to speak with me now? If not, will you have a little bit of time in the next day or two for us to speak?"

"Is this a good time to speak with you? If not, we can reschedule for a better time."

"Did I get you at a bad time?"

"Do you have a few minutes to speak with me now?"

"If you can't take some time to speak with me now, please let me know and we can reschedule at a time that is convenient for you."

3. **Setting expectations.** Let them know what you are looking for—be very specific. You will take the information you completed in your self-analysis and apply it here. Help them visualize what it is you want to do and where it is you want to do it, either by mentioning specific companies, types of companies, or industries of interest. By creating this mental picture for your contact, they can start

thinking of people they know or companies they are aware of that could benefit from being introduced to you. It is very important that you are not vague here. Most people feel they should be broad so they do not limit their opportunities. In reality, that has the opposite effect. It makes it harder for someone to give you a referral. Take a look at these:

"I am looking for an opportunity to work as a sales trader with a publicly-traded financial services company headquartered in the Boston area."

"I am looking to continue practicing law, but work directly for a hospital in a big city such as New York; Chicago; Washington, D.C.; or San Francisco that can take advantage of my malpractice expertise."

"I want to take my executive search experience and look for a senior level position with one of the large outplacement companies such as Lee Hecht Harrison, Drake Beam, or Right Management."

"I want to stay in media as a graphic designer and want to work for a company such as Viacom, AOL, ABC/ESPN, NBC, or a movie studio."

"I am interested in a controller's position with a small to mid-size high-tech firm where they have approximately 50 to 100 people."

4. **Triggering a reaction.** Put their feet to the fire (and maybe flatter them a bit). Here is where you let them know what you want them to do for you. Do you want them to give you some other leads, or names of people for you contact?

Do you want them to take your resume and give it to someone at their company? Do you want them to help you open up a door for you at their company or another company? Remember your call objective and stay focused on what you want to accomplish in this phone call. People have an ego and you are asking for a favor. Don't hesitate to stroke their ego as it may help and they will go further out of their way to help you:

"When we worked together, you were always a great resource. I was hoping you could give me a few names of sales managers you know in pharmaceutical companies locally."

"You are well connected and know everyone in town. Do you know anyone I could speak to about the type of opportunity I've described?"

"I was hoping you could help me out by providing me with contacts I can call in those industries where you would feel comfortable giving me names and phone numbers."

"I noticed that Company X is looking for a person with my credentials, and because you know the owner of the company, I was hoping you could call him on my behalf."

"I'd like you to look at my resume. Perhaps we could get together next Tuesday for lunch and you could tell me what you think? At that time I'd like to pick your brain to see if you could provide me with some ideas of which companies in your industry are ones I should target."

5. **Generating activity.** Your phone call, if managed properly, is going to force your contact to react in some way. They are either going to help or they aren't. If they offer to give you a few names proceed to step 6 (page 115). It's possible they will not be able to give you a name for a variety of reasons. Here are some likely scenarios and how you should respond to them:

A. "I can't think of anyone now."

"This is really important to me. Do you think you can take a few days, reflect on our conversation, and I will call you back at on Friday at 4 p.m. and maybe you will have had time to think of a few people I can contact?"

B. "No."

"Do you mean no you won't help me, or you don't know anyone? As I mentioned before, this is really important to me and I could really use your help."

C. "I don't know anybody that is hiring these days."

"I am not asking you to do any soliciting on my behalf to find out what companies are hiring. I'm really just asking for your help in identifying companies that meet my profile. It's up to me to do the leg work and find out if I would be a good fit."

D. "I have not spoken to Frank in a long time. It would be a stretch for me to call him."

"I'll call. I am really looking for help to open up a door. What's the worst Frank will say when I call him and mention your name? If he says he can't or would not help, I'll just move on. That's the worst that can happen."

6. **Closing the loop:** You got a positive response, so set yourself up for another "warm call." Your contact offers to give you a few names of people they know. Those people are referrals. That's great! Now you want the referral call to go just as well. Part of the reason this last call went well was because of all the preliminary work you did as prescribed in Chapters 1 through 4. The other reason is because you have a solid relationship with the contact. Now you want to get the contact to call the referral on your behalf and start a solid relationship for you with the contact.

This will break the ice and create warm call, making it that much easier for you. Try one of these:

"Do you think you could call Joe on my behalf?"

"Do you think you could call Joe on my behalf, and give him a heads-up so he will be prepared for my call?"

"Do you think you could call Joe on my behalf, and give him a heads-up so he will be prepared for my call? As you know a warm call is more effective than a cold call."

"Do you think you could call Joe on my behalf, and give him a heads up so he will be prepared for my call? As you know a warm call is more effective than a cold call. And your calling him ahead of time makes it that much easier for me to get the conversation started."

Here are two sample phone scripts you can also use as a reference when preparing your own:

Phone Call Script #1:
Lucy, training developer

1. **Set the stage.**

   "Hi Chris, it's Lucy. How have you been? Well, I was recently laid off from Company X and would like to ask for your help."

2. **Make sure you have their undivided attention**

   "Do you have some time to speak with me now? If not, will you have a little bit of time in the next day or two for us to talk?"

3. **Letting them know what you are looking for.**

   "I'm looking for an opportunity to develop training for an established financial services firm in the Chicago area, and my interests lie specifically in developing online training."

4. **Put their feet to the fire and flatter them a bit.**

   "When we worked previously together you were a great resource of information and I was hoping you could help me out by providing me with contact information to the Director of Training at MidAmerica."

5a. **Positive Response—Close the Loop.**

   "As we were talking you mentioned that you knew a few people in the tax department at PWC as well. Would you mind calling them on my behalf?"

   or

   "Thank you. I will call you next week after I speak to (the **Referral**) to let you know how things went."

5b. Negative Response—Trying to turn it around.

"This is really important to me. Would it be possible for you to give this more thought based upon what I am looking for? I would like to call you next Tuesday to see if perhaps you may come up with some ideas. Would that be okay?"

Here is the transcript of Lucy's real life phone call when she used her phone script as a guideline.

CONTACT CALL SCRIPT—LUCY

LUCY:	Hi Chris, it's Lucy. How have you been?
CHRIS:	I'm great. How are you?
LUCY:	Well, I was recently laid off from my company and would like to ask for your help.
	Do you have some time to speak with me now? If not, will you have a little bit of time in the next day or two for us to talk?
CHRIS:	I have time now.
LUCY:	I'm looking for an opportunity in developing training for an established financial services firm in the Chicago area, and my interests lie specifically in developing on-line training.
CHRIS:	Well, online training isn't really my area…
LUCY:	True, however, when we worked previously together you were a great resource of information and I was hoping you could help me out by providing me with contact information to the Director of Training at your company.

CHRIS: Well, sure! I think I just met him at a meeting last week. Let me pull up his name and number for you…His name is Darren Testa….

Here are some last-minute reminders before you create your own script:

- ➤ **Don't use the question, "Do you know any companies looking for people, or are hiring?"** Avoid asking questions that can get an easy no. You risk ending the conversation quickly. Also, you may lose the connection for future requests.

- ➤ **Don't ask people to send your resume to Human Resources.** Your resume will most likely end up in a black hole. Get your resume in the hands of the hiring manger or as high up in the organization as you can go. If your resume eventually does end up in Human Resources, it will have at least been sent there with a strong recommendation that should allow you to stand out from the crowd.

- ➤ **People want to help.** Just ask.

- ➤ **Fear is your friend.** It's okay to be a little nervous calling these people. Stay confident.

- ➤ **Be prepared.** Do not shortcut your due diligence, strategy, or objective for each and every call. Use the previously mentioned guidelines and customize your calls.

Now it's time to create a script for yourself.

PHONE CALL SCRIPT

1. Setting the stage (Getting their attention).

2. Valuing their time.

3. Setting Expectations (Letting them know what you are looking for. Help them start to visualize and think about people they know).

4. Triggering a reaction (Now it's time to put their feet to the fire and also flatter them a little.)

_____

_____

_____

_____

5. Generating an activity.

_____

_____

_____

_____

6. Closing the loop.

_____

_____

_____

_____

Phone Script When Speaking to a Referral

Because you were so effective when speaking with your contacts, they gave you the names of people to call. Now you want to be able to leverage the relationship between the contact and referral and get the referral to meet with you (if that's what you want) or to help you. By managing the conversation correctly, this referral will also become a contact for you as you continue to peel the onion, going through the layers until you get to the core—the right person that can help you.

The way you approach the referral is slightly different from the technique you used when calling your contact. As always, how you conduct yourself when speaking with the referral will leave a lasting impression and directly affect the outcome of your call. In the last chapter, you learned about credibility. Using someone's name to open the door gives you temporary credibility when the conversation gets started. It does not mean this person will definitely help you. Earning more permanent credibility will be dictated by how you conduct yourself throughout the entire phone conversation, which will have a bearing on whether this person will help.

1. **Grabbing the referral's attention.** You need to quickly establish why you are calling. Mentioning your contact's name up front will get the referral to listen to you. You may want to say something such as:

   "You and I have not spoken before. Joel Karlan asked me to give you a call."

   "The reason for my call is your neighbor Melanie and I were talking the other day and she suggested I call you directly."

   "Your brother Jimmy told me to call you."

"Last night I was with Kim Fitzpatrick and she was telling me about you and your company. She suggested I
give you a call."

2. **Valuing their time.** Make sure you have their undivided
attention. Just as you learned about calling your contact,
always ask if this is a good time to talk. You want to
make sure your referrals pay attention to what you say
and that they know it is very important to you. You can't
tell if someone else is in their office, if they are in the
middle of a project, if they might be about to leave the
office to go into a meeting, or any other reasons why they
can not give you the time and attention you need at that
moment.

Here are a few scripts that are slightly different from
what you would say to your contact:

"If for some reason you can't spend a few minutes
with me now, please be candid and we can reched-
ule at a better time."

"Please let me know if this is not a good time for a
discussion and we can reschedule."

"Is this a good time to speak with you? If not, we
can reschedule for a better time."

"Did I get you at a bad time?"

"If you can't take some time to speak with me now,
please let me know and we can reschedule at a
time that is more convenient for you."

3. **Break the tension.** Here is where you bridge your relationship with your contact into an "ice breaker."

"Joel told me to send his regards."

"When was the last time you spoke to Melanie?"

"I hope mentioning Jimmy's name is not going to be the reason you end this call now."

"Frank is a good guy, one of my best friends. I appreciate the fact that he suggested I contact you."

In some instances you may get the question, "What is this about?" Don't let that throw you off your game. Your simple response is:

"Kim told me to call you because…"

4. **Definitive positioning statement.** This is where you talk about your expertise, what you bring to the table, and combine that with your insight into the referrals' companies or industries. This information will give referrals a mental picture of who you are, help them think about how they can help, and who they know that fits the type of company, position, or industry you describe.

You may say:

"My background is 25 years of senior sales and marketing positions in the service business. My expertise is driving revenue and profits. I am bottom-line focused and know how to deliver a favorable ROI. Joel told me a little about your company and after I researched it, I noticed your organization had just been acquired by XYZ company, your largest competitor."

"I've been a customer service representative for the past five years with an electronics distributor, and was recognized every year as the top person in my group. I understand you work with many of the world's leading electronics manufacturers."

"I've been a research analyst for a large commercial real estate firm and they are moving my position out of the area. My boss says I do the work of two people. I want to stay local with a quality real estate firm."

5. **Setting expectations.** Here is where you ask for their help. This part of the call should start with "I need your help," or "I could use your help."

"I need your help. I am interested in working for your company and would like your help in introducing me to the right person to speak to about an opportunity."

"I could use your help. I am interested in pursuing an opportunity in this industry and Kevin told me you would be a good contact to network with."

"I could use your help. I am interested in pursuing an opportunity in this industry and Greg said you may be able to provide me with a few names of companies or individuals I should speak with."

"Josie told me you were well connected and I should introduce myself to you. I could really use your help."

"I need your help. Betsy told me you were the most knowledgeable person she knew in this area and said you were the best person for me to contact."

6. **Triggering a reaction.** Generating an activity. Most importantly, remember what your call objective is. What do you want to this person to do for you? Here is where you ask for the order.

"I would appreciate it if you could give me the names of some people you know whom I could speak to about my search."

"I would appreciate it if you could connect me with Bill Waldman at S-Drive."

"Could you send my resume to Fran Jenkins at ASP?"

"I would welcome the chance to meet you in person. Perhaps you could give me some leads."

"Do you think you could help me identify the right people in your industry?"

"Do you mind if I call you back again in one week's time after you've had a chance to look at my resume? At that time, we can discuss this further and it allows you some time to think of other people I should contact."

Sample Referral Script

1. **Grab their attention.**

   "Hi, Melissa. This is Stacy McDonald. Chris Dunn suggested I give you a call.

2. **Value their time.**

   "Did I catch you at a good time? Great!"

3. **Break the tension.**

   "Chris and I had dinner Monday. He told me to send you his regards. He said he was a friend of yours. How do you know him?"

4. **Definitive Positioning Statement.**

"I have been an Account Executive for The Clarke advertising company in their local office. Chris told me a little bit about what's happening in your company. I did some additional research and learned that your company is expanding in the western suburbs. I am known for having excellent customer relationships and maintain the highest client retention rate in the company."

5. **Setting expectations—the purpose for the call.**

"I would be interested in speaking with the person in your company that is going to be heading up that new office."

6. **Triggering a reaction. Generate an activity (ask for the order).**

"Do you think you could help me get in contact with the right person?"

Now it's time to create a referral script for yourself.

REFERRAL PHONE SCRIPT

1. Grab their attention.

_____

_____

_____

_____

2. Value their time.

_____

_____

_____

_____

3. Break the tension.

_____

_____

_____

_____

_____

_____

4. Definitive Positioning Statement.

_____

_____

_____

_____

5. Setting expectations—the purpose for the call.

_____

_____

_____

_____

_____

6. Triggering a reaction.

_____

_____

_____

_____

_____

Give Yourself Some Feedback

Your conversation will lead to some sort of reaction. What this means is that another activity or action will follow based on the particulars of that call. After your phone call is complete, you need to go review this checklist before you pick up the phone to make additional calls.

- ❏ What was your call objective?
- ❏ Did you make it easy for this person to help you?
- ❏ Did you remember not to "let them off the hook?"
- ❏ Did they commit to do something for you?
- ❏ Was the call objective satisfied?

If you can put a check next to each question—good. But you still have more work to do.

Throughout this process of calling people and peeling the onion, pay attention to what's being said to you during the conversation. Sometimes the person you contact does not respond the way you expected, and you may start to doubt the strength of the relationship. Don't sweat it. Focus not just on what they're saying, but on remembering the importance of listening.

> *"We are amazed but not amused by all the things you said you would do."*
>
> —Stevie Wonder

You read about the importance of following through and following up in the previous chapter. Whatever needs to be done, make sure you live up to each of your commitments. This will speak volumes about what kind of long-lasting credibility you will have with referrals, which will go a long way towards determining how big and how strong your SuperNetwork will become. You are constantly being evaluated based upon what you say and do. Take care of business.

Leave Voice Mail That Gets Their Attention

Any voice mail message needs to be brief, peak your recipient's interest, be informative, and trigger an action. The type you leave for a contact will be different from the type you leave for a referral. These are time-tested examples that get people to either call you back or prepare them to receive your next call. Either way, these will guarantee that you will be speaking to them soon.

Leave voice mail for contacts

"Dan, this is Joanna. I need to speak with you about a private matter. I will call you tonight at home around 8 p.m."

"Dan, this is Joanna. I need to speak with you. Could you please call me when you get back to the office?"

"Dan. This is Joanna. It's important to me that we connect before the week is out. I will try you again tomorrow morning. If that doesn't work for you, please let me know what's good for you."

Leave voice mail for a referrals

"Hi Frank. This is Len Steckler. Jane Peterson suggested I call you. It is important to me that we connect. If you can call me back at 4 p.m. today I would appreciate it. My number is 602-555-1234. If that's not good for you, I will call you back on Friday at 10 a.m."

"Hi Frank. This is Len Stecker. I am calling at Jane Peterson's request. I would appreciate it if we could talk within the next two days. You can reach me at 602-555-1234. I am available between 3 p.m. and 5 p.m. today, and 10 a.m. and 4 p.m. tomorrow. If I have not heard from you I will call you back on Friday at 10 a.m."

Hi Frank. I was recently with Len Steckler and he told me to call you directly. I could use your help. I can be reached at 602-867-0980 all day today. If I have not heard from you in a few days, I will call you back on Friday at 10 AM."

Gatekeepers: The Administrators Who Keep You Away From the Person You Want to Speak With

It's important to develop some rapport with these individuals. Ask for their name and let them know you really need their help. This will disarm most. If that does not work, mentioning your contact or referral's name should neutralize them. They generally have no idea how well your contact or referral knows the person you are trying to reach, or the relationship between them. The "gatekeeper" is fear-driven. Using this knowledge will get you what you need.

I've been working with a defense contractor for the last six months. The Vice President of Administration, Ellen, is someone I have known for more than 20 years. Linda, Ellen's assistant, did a thorough job of screening my initial call. When I told her about my long relationship with Ellen, her tone and demeanor changed. Now when I call, she immediately recognizes my voice, and we have developed a relationship of our own. The power of using the contact or referral's name will help you get through, too.

Here are a few that work:

"Please let Frank know that this is Alex Herman calling at the request of Joel Karlan, who wants us to connect. Please ask him to call me tomorrow at 10 a.m. at 202-555-1200."

or

"I could really use your help. What's the best time and day for me to call him back? My call carries a degree of urgency and it is important that we speak."

TRANSCRIPT OF LUCY'S CONVERSATION WITH A "GATEKEEPER"

ADMIN. ASST.: Hello, Darren Testa's office.

LUCY: Hello, this is Lucy White calling. Is Darren available?

ADMIN. ASST.: No, Darren isn't available right now. May I ask what this is in reference to?

LUCY: Please let Darren know that this is Lucy White calling at the request of Chris Tanner. If you could let Darren know that Chris wanted us to connect, that would be great. Please have him call me tomorrow at 10 a.m. at 412-555-1200.

ADMIN. ASST.: I'm not sure that he will be available at that time, but I'll give him the message.

LUCY: I appreciate that. My call carries a degree of urgency and it is important that we speak. I could really use your help. When is the best time of day for me to call him back?

ADMIN. ASST.: You can try back tomorrow at 8 a.m. He's usually around to take phone calls at that time.

LUCY: Thank you very much. I'll call back tomorrow.

ADMIN. ASST.: Thank you.

Did you notice how the administrator's tone changed as a result of Lucy's approach? The administrator was not going to cause a problem when Lucy said, "it's important." Use this transcript as a guideline if you find yourself speaking with a tough administrator.

When a Link in Your SuperNetwork Doesn't Perform

What happens when you reach the right person and you get the cold shoulder? Sometimes you will have what you thought was a great conversation with a referral and (for whatever reason) the referral has not responded the way you had hoped. Here are a few likely scenarios:

1. You called the referral and you have not spoken directly with him yet. You have left a few messages without receiving a call back.

2. You spoke to the referral and she was in a rush, told you she would call you back and you are still waiting for the call. Or she scheduled a specific time to speak to you again and you feel you were "blown off."

3. You spoke to the referral and he promised to do something for you (send your resume along to

someone else, or call someone else on your behalf), and he has not followed through on his
commitment.

4. You are speaking with the referral and your instincts tell you things are not going well. You are
getting a bad vibe. And by the time you are off
the phone, your gut is telling you this person is
not going to help you.

Is it me or is it the referral?

It is natural for you to wonder if the problem is with the
referral or with yourself. You'll probably find yourself re-
flecting back on the call and trying to figure out if you did
something wrong or didn't handle things right.

Don't doubt yourself yet. There's a good chance you
didn't do anything wrong at all. It could be that the referral
has been traveling, or has been out sick and unable to get back
to you in a timely manner. Perhaps their boss imposed some
deadlines, or they just forgot even though they made a commitment to you. There are any number of things that could be
going on in the referral's life that could impact your referral's
ability to help you.

What should I do?

Go back to your contact that gave you the referral. Explain the situation and ask that person to call the referral on
your behalf to find out what happened. This will give you clarification on what happened and an opportunity to get things
back on track. This will also give you closure. If it was not *you*
that was the problem, the referral will be primed for your follow-up call. If in fact there *was* something you did during the
conversation that alienated the referral, learn from it and make
sure you don't repeat the mistake. Then move on.

Once you have prepared your own customized scripts, you are ready to get on the phone and make things happen. You now know:

➤ How to prepare an effective script when speaking with contacts, referrals, and gatekeepers.

➤ What to say and how to ask for help.

➤ How to present yourself in a way that will get the contact or referral to put you in touch with not just anyone, but the "right" person that can help you.

➤ How to leave an effective voice mail message that will get a return call.

➤ Know what to do when someone gives you the "cold shoulder."

Now you'd probably prefer to hear the phone message Diane left on Dr. Hartley's voice mail for the radiographer position at the children's hospital.

"Hello, Dr. Hartley. Dr. Narweigh at Chicago Children's, whom I think you know, said I was the best radiographer for children he had ever seen. Your HR people told me I need to be okayed by you before they can hire me, so when can I meet with you to discuss your vacancy? My name's Diane Bright and I can be reached anytime on my cell phone at 805-555-5555. Thanks."

These scripts are going to lead to great conversations. If you have been following along and have not cut any corners, you are going to get people to help, and you will be getting closer to the "right" person.

This is getting exciting isn't it?

The Perfect
Mentor:

Find a World-class Boss

A rtie scanned the updated contact lists that he had printed out. Jake was right—following his phone scripts carefully really made a difference, and it had been a productive week. Artie had not only tracked down a great job in which he could build on his experience in pharmaceutical sales—he had even been able to get an interview scheduled. Plus, he had some new contacts and leads on other promising jobs. What an improvement over last week! Artie had made a lot of calls that week too, but his mentor Jake had pointed out that he wasn't staying "on task"—he was having some really enjoyable chats but his search was not progressing. So this week Artie had carefully prepared for every call, stuck to the scripts, and had not forgotten his action items! These weekly talks with Jake were really keeping him focused on his goals.

Realistically, once you start executing your plan, you are going to get very busy and will need some help to keep track of your progress. In order for this *SuperNetworking* plan to succeed, you must find a mentor to report to and meet with formally on a weekly basis. This mentor will serve as your boss and hold you accountable to qualitative and quantitative measures. At the end of this chapter, you will review a mentor selection criteria checklist to show you how to select the right person for you.

Why Is It Important to Have a Mentor?

If your boss told you that he needed a project completed by 5 p.m. tomorrow, no questions asked, there is a 99.9 percent chance that you will deliver on time. Now, if you were your own boss and missed the same deadline, you would probably tell yourself, "I think I'll finish it tomorrow." Having a mentor will force you to live up to your commitments.

A mentor helps formalize this process. Once the plan goes into effect, you will become busy with letters, phone calls, follow ups, and meetings. Things could start falling through the cracks, and this is where most job search plans fail. Just as with some diets, you start out with good intentions, but over time you can get distracted, begin to cheat a little, saying to yourself, "I'll go back on it tomorrow." But tomorrow never happens and you do not stay on course. A mentor will keep you on track. Having a scheduled weekly meeting at a set time will give this part of the process the structure and discipline required to stay the course.

Here is just one example of how a good mentor can help you. You may think you have a job all "locked up." You stop making the extra phone calls and sending out your resume. A good mentor eliminates that temptation and knows you cannot stop the process until you have accepted an offer.

Your mentor will formalize the process and hold you accountable, keeping you focused until you have truly secured a new job.

Why Can't I Have More Than Just One Mentor?

Listening to more than one person can get confusing. It's very hard to reach consensus when you are looking for a job and so many people want to offer advice. You are bound to hear different opinions. Also, if you don't follow a person's advice, they might get upset with you because you did not listen to them. You can't win this way. Having one person to speak with about your search eliminates the danger of trying to satisfy too many masters. Don't worry about hurting their feelings. Follow the plan you create with your mentor. By listening to one person, you will have continuity in the way you handle each situation.

What Will a Mentor Do For Me?

A mentor will give you objectivity and help you make intelligent and informed decisions. The mentor will serve as a sounding board for you. You may come up with what appears to be a great idea. The mentor will let you know if it makes sense, is reality based, and has a good chance for success. The mentor will help you crystallize your thoughts and give you additional ideas to consider. A mentor will help give you the confidence that you need.

Looking for your next opportunity can be a lonely process. It also will give you tremendous highs and lows. When things are hectic and you are sending out tons of resumes, interviewing a lot, and making new connections, you will feel great. When things are not going as well as you planned, a sense of panic can set in. Having a mentor to work with will give you a sense of comfort and stability during what could be a roller coaster ride of emotions. Here are some important things a mentor will do for you:

➤ Give you the objectivity you need to make good, informed decisions about your career.

➤ Formalize the process and help you stay focused.

➤ Force you to work the plan consistently to maximize your opportunities.

➤ Be honest with you and hold you accountable when your performance is falling short.

➤ Pick you up when you are down, give you words of encouragement, and pump you up when you need it.

➤ Stay with you until you land your dream job.

Part of the mentor's role is qualitative as well as quantitative. The mentor will also be available to help you with your strategy, role playing, letter writing, e-mails, elevator pitch, and phone scripts.

Your mentor will keep you on your toes. A good mentor will provide encouragement, but also apply appropriate pressure when needed. Maintaining that sort of balance is very important throughout the process.

What Will a Mentor Expect From Me?

Even though you have a personal connection with this person and your mentor is volunteering their time to help you, do not forget what role they serve in this process. You need to treat this person as you would a boss. As you prepare for all conversations with your mentor they will expect you to conduct yourself in a professional manner. He or she will be treating this like the business situation it is and you should, too.

Your mentor will have certain expectations. Here is what you need to do to keep your mentor engaged in this process:

> ➤ **Show weekly progress.** During your scheduled weekly meeting, be prepared to discuss qualitative and quantitative aspects of your progress, which should bring you closer to your dream job in an accelerated timeline.

> ➤ **Honesty.** Tell the truth to your mentor. It's the best way he or she can help you.

> ➤ **Live up to your commitment.** Deliver on your promises.

> ➤ **Put forth a Herculean effort.** This plan is hard work. Don't cheat yourself or your mentor.

> ➤ **Focus.** You can easily get distracted. Endure the course you set out on with your mentor and do not deviate from the plan unless you mutually agree to a specific change.

> ➤ **Don't waste your mentor's time.** He or she is doing you a favor.

What's In It For the Mentor?

The right mentor wants to see you happy and in the job you want. Your mentor cares about doing what is necessary to contribute to your success in landing your next job. Mentors want to contribute in a small way and do not expect anything in return. They are not looking for a monetary award.

They will be happy for you, but also will feel good about themselves for their good deed. I am sure that when they consider your request for help, they will think back to when other people helped them in their lives. Everyone has gotten help from others along the way. Helping you is an opportunity for them to give something back. Here is what your mentor wants (if your mentor is looking for anything else, you have the wrong person):

- Satisfaction from having an impact.

- Satisfaction from being capable of accomplishing what was asked.

- Recognition.

- Acknowledgement.

- Appreciation.

How Do I Ask Someone to Be My Mentor?

Most job seekers find this to be a difficult task. I realize there is great apprehension associated with this because you are about to ask someone close to you to get intimately involved in a process that is very important to you.

Once you identify the right person, just follow this outline and script, and you will get commitment from your mentor. This person is out there. You just have to ask.

Elements of a Successful Script

- Value their time.

- Explain the situation.

- Express that you value their time and opinion.

➤ Ask for their help.

➤ Describe the mentoring process.

ASKING A MENTOR SCRIPT

1. **Value their time.**

    HERMAN: Natalie, do you have a minute?

    NATALIE: Yes I do.

2. **Explain the situation.**

    HERMAN: As you know, I am looking for my next job opportunity. This is the most important thing to me right now. I have a very strategic approach to my search. Part of the plan is that I need to select a mentor, a coach in the process who will keep me on the straight and narrow.

3. **Express that you value their time and opinion.**

    HERMAN: I think you know how much I respect you and admire you.

    NATALIE: Thank you very much.

4. **Ask for their help.**

    HERMAN: I would like to talk to you about being my mentor in this process.

    NATALIE: I am flattered that you would want me. What do I need to do?

5. Describe the mentoring process.

HERMAN: In essence, you would be my boss in this
process and stay with the program until
I start my new job. You would need to
meet with me formally one day per week
at a prescribed day and time and we
would review my progress. There are
weekly progress forms I would submit
to you and we would be discussing my
results in a quantitative and qualitative
way. In addition, if things come up
during the week, I would be able to call
you to ask for advice. What do you
think so far?

NATALIE: You still have my interest. Tell me
more.

If your mentor is still interested, you should continue by
referring to what a mentor does and what the mentor should
expect from you.

After you explained that part of the process and the say
yes, suggest that you get together immediately. At that time,
you can show your mentor this book so he or she can understand the process and the weekly progress report (which is in
Chapter 7) to get a better understanding of the depth of the
program, and how the mentor fits in. (And yes, you can even
let your mentor read this chapter. You can share a good laugh
about the power of a scripted conversation.)

Criteria for Selecting a Mentor

As you start thinking about who in your life might be a
good mentor, there are certain characteristics you should
look for. Here are the essential ingredients:

➤ Trustworthy.

➤ Candor.

➤ Accepting of your wins and losses.

➤ Highly-available.

➤ Willing to push you and stay with you through difficult times.

➤ Gives praise and criticism.

➤ Objective.

➤ Has high standards.

➤ Enthusiastic about your success.

Who should I consider choosing?

Now that you have identified the qualities of a good mentor, you need to start thinking about who is right for you.

You need to select someone to who you are comfortable telling things that might be embarrassing—maybe you are not meeting your goals or maybe you perceive a flaw in yourself that you need to overcome. These are things you need to share with your mentor. The right mentor will give you the support you need at the appropriate time to persevere.

There are people in your life to whom you may be very close, but who would not be the right mentor. One example is your significant other. He or she certainly has an enormous interest in seeing you work, but may not be as objective as you would like. Your mate being your mentor can frequently lead to an uncomfortable situation. The job search is a formal act, and the relationship with your mentor should be as well.

Here are some suggestions for people who you may want to consider:

- ➤ **Former bosses.** They know you and probably know what you are capable of. They have already been your boss before and they know how to motivate you.

- ➤ **Former colleague.** They also know what you are capable of and could provide solid advice and speak to you "as if they are in your shoes."

- ➤ **Siblings or cousins.** They are your family, and family generally has an unwavering commitment to you win, lose, or draw. Their sense of loyalty and commitment to you and the process will be very strong.

- ➤ **Close friends.** Just like siblings or cousins, they have the same motivation to help you.

- ➤ **Spouses.** Some people would select this person for the obvious reasons—they have a vested interest. They are in tune and very aware of what's going on and the importance of getting a new job quick. They are the person you confide in about most everything. They probably know you better than anyone else. It's a close call. The only danger is that they may be too close to the situation and you may feel additional pressure.

- ➤ **Neighbors.** They do not have the emotional investment as some of the others mentioned do, but they certainly care about you and want you to be successful.

Some others to consider are: a friends of the family who have experience in your field, superiors from work that are not in your department, people from your religious organization, or a person you met through business and became friendly with.

Who shouldn't I choose?

There might be people in your life that on the surface look like a potential mentor, but after you conduct a thorough diagnostic, you should realize they are not the best person for you. Here are some people that you should avoid and why:

- **Current boss.** Obviously you do not want to let this person know you are looking.

- **Role models.** A role model is someone you admire, look up to, emulate, and find yourself modeling your life after. These people may try to mold you to be like them. They might be tempted to pressure you to make decisions based on their needs, which may not be in your best interest.

- **Someone in a similar position personally or professionally.** A person who is also looking for a job can not give you the objectivity you need. He or she may become jealous of your successes along the way or breach your confidence in order to help him- or herself. If this person is not making any progress on his or her search, he or she may pull you down too. Misery does love company. Avoid this person.

- **Anyone expecting a monetary award.** If someone asks you, "How much will you pay me for my time and commitment?" you have the wrong person.

MENTOR SELECTION TOOL

Mentor Candidate (name)													
Positive Qualities	Trust												
	Candor												
	Acceptance												
	Availability												
	Pushes you												
	Gives Praise and criticism												
	Objective												
	Sets high standards												
	Enthusiastic												
Negative Qualities	Current boss												
	Role model												
	In similar position												
	Expects money												
	Too close to me												

➤ **Anyone too close to you.** Some of the best people on the surface may not be the ones you want to speak to about your search. This relationship requires total candor. You will be discussing private and confidential matters, and you need to know that the mentor can handle it. If you are not comfortable discussing these things with your spouse, siblings, or close friends, they are probably not the right ones for you.

➤ **Yourself.** You can not be your own. You need someone who is objective, and you can't be. This plan will fail if you choose yourself.

Listed on page 148 is a mentor selection tool. Based on what you have learned in this chapter, fill in the top line with a person you think may fit the criteria previously discussed. Now go through this list and put a check mark in the areas you feel best describes this individual. It should become clear who the best mentor candidates arc for you.

By the end of this exercise, you should have identified a few people whom you would consider asking to be your mentor. You need to select someone in order for *SuperNetworking* to work the way it was intended. This program functions only in a building-block format. You need to complete this chapter before you can go forward.

The Accountability Factor:

*Track Your Progress
and Results*

After hanging up the phone, Sandra sat back and took a deep breath. When George O'Neill's secretary had called to say that he was on the line, she had been taken completely by surprise. She flipped open her notebook computer and in a few seconds found the file she was looking for—the one with her phone script, the research about George and his law firm, and all her questions for him. Not bad, considering that she hadn't been expecting the call. True, she had spoken to some of his partners, but Bob was known to be a tough nut to crack. And now she had an appointment with him for next week! "This database is invaluable," she thought. "Not only is it keeping me organized, it's really helping me impress my contacts.

The days of jotting down the name of a referral on a loose piece of paper or storing everything in your head about a previous conversation are over. You need one place to keep track of what was said and what actions are required. Being organized is critical to the success of SuperNetworking, and that's why you must build and maintain a personal networking database.

The importance of developing and maintaining a database of your network of contacts cannot be overemphasized. And not just for getting your next job, but for your life in general. When your job plan is fully launched, you will be at the early stages of building a strong network. Over time, the contacts you make and information you gain will improve your quality of life. Being able to access the best pediatrician when they are telling others that they're not taking any new patients, or having a contact to get you tickets to a sold-out event are simple examples of how life will be when you constantly maintain your network of contacts.

It is up to you to drive this process. The strength and size of your network is going to be a reflection of the amount of time and effort you put into it. By keeping track of your network of personal contacts, you will be in control of managing your search, which will give you confidence and make this a positive experience.

Keeping Track of Your Progress

It is important that you set up specific fields in your SuperNetworking database so you can easily access your data. This will save you time when an important phone call comes in, or when you are reviewing who you should call back on what particular day.

Your efficiency will be greatly enhanced by investing in your personal network database. But as with a bank account, you must keep your database in order. If you do not put anything in, you won't get anything out. If you don't keep track of your progress here, and you let things slip through the cracks, you are not going to get as much out of this program as you should. You must take the time to capture all the information in one place.

Critical Database Information

The key fields of information to capture in every phone call are in the following list. Some of the fields were discussed in Chapter 2 when you put your initial contact list together. Now that the process is moving forward, you will have contacts and referrals to call and you'll need to add some more fields to organize your database in a way that makes it easy for you to manage the process.

This database structure has been designed to help you stay focused on what is truly important and eliminate the minutia. The critical fields are:

➤ **Contact name:** This is the person you are calling.

➤ **Title (if known):** Mr./Ms./Mrs./Dr. If you have this information before your call, great. If not, it would help if you ask during the conversation.

➤ **Company name:** Be sure to have the correct spelling.

➤ **Phone number:** Again, attention to this type of detail is very important.

➤ **E-mail address:** Many things can go wrong here. In order to make sure you captured this information correctly, repeat it to your contact.

➤ **Referred by:** This would be the person (contact) who told you to call. This is your door opener to beginning the warm call.

➤ **Date of contact:** Enter the date for every communication you have.

➤ **Date for follow-up:** As discussed throughout *SuperNetworking,* every call should lead to some future activity. This will help you keep track of when you have to execute an activity on a specific day.

➤ **Resume sent:** This way you can keep track of where, when, and to whom you sent your resume.

➤ **Interview set up:** This will help you manage your schedule and see what type of progress you are making.

➤ **Status:** This will give you a quick synopsis of where things stand with this individual.

➤ **Action:** This will let you know what is supposed to happen next.

➤ **Thank-you note sent:** As stated earlier, people like to be asked and thanked. Let them know you appreciate what they have done or will be doing for you in the future. This field can be set up with either a check, or a "yes" or "no."

➤ **Comments:** Here is a field where you can put additional information that did not fit into the other fields. You may learn something in your initial conversation that will have relevance in the future. Capture that information here.

I am sure you have heard the expression "sales is a numbers game." I agree. Over time, the numbers always bear this out. Just like a salesperson, you have a goal to land your next job in less than 30 days. A salesperson's goal would be the quota. If either of you only focused on your end result and do not understand what it will take to get there, you will generally fail. For the salesperson, missing quota is a recipe for termination. For you it could mean a much lengthier and more painful job search.

Stay focused on the process and the results will take care of themselves. If you complete a little bit of the process each day, you'll be in your new job before you know it.

If the sales person's pipeline is dry, they will have a difficult time making quota. If they have lots of activity in the funnel, chances are they will reach their quota. Keep your funnel full of meaningful activity and good things will happen for you.

In one of my workshops, we were reviewing this section of the program when an unemployed software engineer said, "This is hard work—how much time should I put into this?" I asked him what else he had going on, and what the most important thing to him was now. The obvious answer was his getting back to work. I told him that the more time he dedicated to reaching his weekly measurements, the sooner he *would* be back to work. He e-mailed me three weeks later to let me know our conversation was a turning point for him. He had focused on meeting all his numbers, and that day he had accepted an offer from a company to which he was referred by a contact he met at the workshop.

I stated at the beginning that this is hard work, there are no shortcuts to success, and building a SuperNetwork takes time and effort. For the people that think it is too tough: You are the ones who will rationalize why you did not reach their numbers. For the individuals who constantly exceed weekly expectations: You will be in your dream job sooner than you ever expected. You make the choice.

Weekly Progress Report: Your Mentor Wants Your Numbers

Accountability and responsibility are essential elements that guarantee you will find your next job quickly. Before each regularly scheduled meeting with your mentor you will be responsible for preparing a weekly report that tracks your progress and provides a reality check on where you are relative to your goals and objectives. The information in your database will be used as a reference point when you work with your mentor during the *qualitative* portion of your weekly discussions.

Your database will also help you in preparing for the *quantitative* portion of your weekly meeting. These are specific numbers-based performance standards with clear benchmarks of critical success factors. Those are the numbers you need to stay focused on reaching every week. Your mentor will hold you accountable to these measurements.

The uniqueness of the *SuperNetworking* program is the combination of having a mentor to serve as your boss and having a numbers-based system with set standards to track your progress and results. By achieving these specific numbers-based standards every week, you *will* see immediate results.

Having to present documentation that reports your progress should bring back memories. Whether it was bringing home your report card, or meeting with your boss on a weekly basis, we have all been in these situations. You have to show someone what you have done and it's much more powerful if it's there in black and white. It can be pretty sobering, but it will help push you. You won't want to be embarrassed by submitting a less than favorable report card on yourself, especially when you have so much to gain or lose.

Once you know what the standards are and understand and embrace the concept, you will be on your way to a speedy and successful job search. Ed Koch, former Mayor of New York, used to go around the city asking people, "How am I doing?" Well, this is the documentation that lets your mentor know how you are doing.

The standards of performance and critical success factors set forth are based on time-tested results. They will give you a Return on Investment (ROI), which will be your payoff from all your hard work.

Standards of Performance

➤ **Unacceptable performance.** If you maintain numbers at this level it will take you an inordinate amount of time until you land your next job. That's a fact.

➤ **Acceptable performance.** These are the bare minimum numbers you should achieve. These are clearly the departure point numbers. If you are consistently on the high end, you will find yourself busy and getting closer to landing your dream job.

➤ **Exceptional performance.** If you are reaching these numbers, you will be in your dream job quickly—sooner than you ever would have imagined. You will probably have a few options too. I was the mentor for Hank, the technical support professional that was mentioned in the Introduction. We only met for three weeks. He was consistently exceeding expectations and was back to work within four weeks.

Critical Success Factors

➤ **Number of calls made.** It all starts with making the initial call to get this process rolling. You have developed at least 40 names from the initial contact list. When you start talking to more people, you will start developing more connections, which will open up more doors for you. If you are using the scripts properly, you should have plenty of calls to make.

➤ **Number of new contacts established.** We've learned that as you peel the onion, you generally should get two additional referrals. You should have enough people in your contact list to make many warm calls and get you closer to the right person.

➤ **Number of resumes sent.** This is a field that can be very misleading. It's just as much quality as quantity. However, like sales, it is a numbers game and the more you have in the pipeline, the better your chances are of landing quickly.

➤ **Number of interviews set up.** If you are scheduling interviews, you are getting closer to your goal. Everybody wants to hit a home run. In order to hit your home run, you need to get into the batter's box. That's what the interviews will do for you—get you up to the plate.

➤ **Number of in-person interviews.** If you have many in-person interviews scheduled, you are getting close to starting your new job. The difference between *in-person interviews* and *interviews scheduled* is that you may schedule one this week, but it might not take place for a few weeks.

Now you know what your objectives are. Listed on page 161 are the actual numbers, the milestones you need to reach on a weekly basis.

Forecast

Here are the numbers that you will be measured against and held accountable for. (See page 161.) Notice that the "number of offers received" field is blank. The reason is because you need to stay focused on the five other fields on a daily basis and reach the exceptional levels on a weekly basis. These are the activities that will drive your process. If you stay committed to achieving exceptional numbers, the offers will follow.

Actual

These are the actual numbers you will enter on a weekly basis to be used when meeting with your mentor. (See page 161.) You are on the honor system here. If you inflate your numbers, you are only kidding yourself. This information can easily be taken from the information entered into your database.

Your mentor will help you raise the bar and push you to constantly exceed expectations. The mentor will also be objective when looking at your weekly statistics. When I was working with Hank, I noticed that he was at an unacceptably low level of calls, but at an exceptional level for new contacts established and interviews set up. He explained that his calls to referrals using a contact's name were working well. He was getting a lot of warm responses and was having great success converting these contacts into interviews.

I reminded him that even though he was having success, he could not afford to get complacent and think he did not have to do all the other components of the search. He agreed.

When he came back the following week, most of the numbers in his report were identical to the week before. The exception was that the number of in-person interviews had increased. Even though he was at unacceptable levels in two areas, he was at exceptional levels in three. By our third week, he was pretty sure an offer was coming within days. I reminded him I would still hold him accountable to these measurements when we met the next week. I also pointed out he should not assume he had the job, and he should not stop this process until he signs an offer letter. Three days later, he called to tell me he did receive an offer. We discussed the particulars of the offer and the next day he went to the company's local office, accepted the position, and signed the offer letter.

If you stay focused on the process and consistently exceed your weekly objectives, the results will take care of themselves. You will get your new job faster, just like Hank did.

If you cannot measure it, you cannot manage it.
—Paul Kazarian, Investment Banking
Professional

ACCOUNTABILITY AND RESPONSIBILITY—WEEKLY PROGRESS FORECAST	Number of Calls Per Week	Number of New Contacts Established	Number of Resumes Sent	Number of In-person Interviews	Number of Interviews Set Up	Number of Offers Received
UNACCEPTABLE	25	5	10	0–2	0–1	
ACCEPTABLE	26–50	6–14	11–15	3–5	2–4	
EXCEPTIONAL	MORE THAN 51	MORE THAN 15	MORE THAN 16	MORE THAN 6	MORE THAN 5	

ACCOUNTABILITY AND RESPONSIBILITY—WEEKLY PROGRESS REPORT

	Number of Calls Per Week	Number of New Contacts Established	Number of Resumes Sent	Number of In-person Interviews	Number of Interviews Set Up	Number of Offers Received
WEEK 1						
WEEK 2						
WEEK 3						
WEEK 4						
WEEK 5						
WEEK 6						
WEEK 7						
WEEK 8						

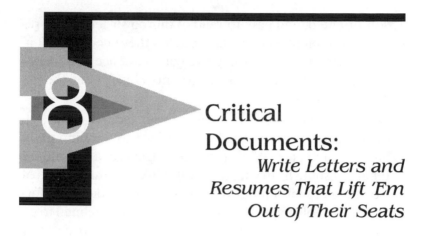

Critical Documents:
Write Letters and Resumes That Lift 'Em Out of Their Seats

Dan had finally located a great job after building his network—an opportunity to break into a top-of-line company in the food services industry. When the Vice President of operations asked him to send a resume and a letter outlining his qualifications, he didn't hesitate for a minute. "No problem!" Dan said to himself. Dan had probed during the conversation and learned what was important to the hiring manager. He was excited about this opportunity and now he knew how to craft a letter that would really make him stand out from the competition.

Over the past two decades, I have reviewed thousands of cover letters and resumes. My strongest advice to you is to customize all of your correspondence. In my previous career as an executive recruiter, I grew to appreciate a strong resume that was tailored to my client's company or industry, action-oriented, and easy to read. Your cover letter and re-sume are similar to your elevator pitch—they need to work in less than 60 seconds. If you capture your audience's attention, they'll read further. If not, it will go into a black hole, the file with countless others.

Dan was able to prepare an effective response because he had asked good questions and learned what was truly important to his target audience. When hiring managers get a customized letter and resume from you, they will think you are the type of person their organization could use. If these contacts or refer-rals are favorably impressed, they will be more inclined to go out of their way to help you either inside or outside their company.

When you are asked to send a resume and cover letter, it is likely you will be competing with others. Sometimes your natural reaction to this may be negative, thinking that they'll never be able to sort through everyone. You need to realize that in order to separate yourself, you have to deal with the target audience's perception of what's truly important in the credentials of the candidate they want to hire. Once you are programmed to respond this way, you will be ready to craft a document that is different from the others.

Cover Letters

Many people go to the Internet and use boilerplate cover letters to create their own. You can recognize these a mile away. If you are using them, *stop now*. At least 75 percent of your competition is doing this and their letters have the same look from the header all the way through the content and sign-off. The only differences are in the words.

During the last recession, I was the Vice President of Sales and Marketing for the country's third largest privately-held security firm. I needed to hire a new Marketing Director.

We received over 400 responses. The ones that came from referrals and contacts immediately went to the top of the pile. Unfortunately none of these people were qualified. The Human Resource Manager provided me with the top 50 candidates and asked me to review their paperwork and select five people to interview. There was just one cover letter that stood out from the rest. This candidate put together a list of the top 10 reasons why I should hire her. Here were her reasons:

#10. Knowledge of and experience working in the security business.

#9. Experienced in working for privately-held organizations.

#8. Experienced in creating and managing direct mail, developing collateral material, and corporate identity programs.

#7. Dedicated to customer satisfaction both internal and external.

#6. Very hungry—I want this job.

#5. Excellent sense of humor and gets along well with others.

#4. Proficient in Windows and MAC environments.

#3. Interested in finding a home—the right place—with long-term growth potential.

#2. I believe your company is best in its class and I could help create effective messaging to get the word out to your target markets.

#1. Interview me and you will not regret it.

This person immediately stood out from the crowd because of her cover letter. Her resume was not as strong, but I thought if she were that creative when it came to getting in the door, she might be worth my time. This person was one of the five finalists and eventually became my Marketing Director. Push yourself to be creative and you too can stand out from the pack.

Your cover letter

The cover letter is merely a door opener, but you should treat it as the most important document you will send to your target audience. Some people do not even read the resume unless the cover letter piques their interest.

Sometimes you will be creating a cover letter because you are responding to an opening. Other times you are making people aware of your talent in the hope of creating an opportunity. Either way, be sure somewhere in the cover letter you clearly articulate what you want the target audience to do with the attached resume. This will remind your contacts and referrals of why you are writing to them and will make it easy for them to help you.

Avoid being bland. Spice things up. Here are the things you must consider before you create any cover letter:

Do your homework

As you already know, you need to find out as much as you can about the person, company, specific job (if that is what you are responding to), or hiring manager before you put pen to paper. This information may come from your due diligence or possibly the latest call you had with a particular person. Either way, you must understand as much as possible about who you are corresponding with and what you are corresponding about. It is very important that you understand and react to what is truly important to your target audience. Be prepared to respond in kind to what they perceive as important to them, not *your* perception of what is important.

Customize

Make sure you accentuate your strengths as they pertain to your target audience's hot buttons or what the hiring company is looking for. For example, if the company is looking for a controller who has pharmaceutical experience and you have it, be sure to list your accomplishments in this field. Also the controller applicant would want to show how the company would benefit from the applicant's pharmaceutical experience in the cover letter. When your target audience is reading your cover letter, they should be able to start developing a mental picture of you and how your experience relates to their needs.

If you are a controller and your contacts ask for your resume because they want to let referrals know about you, then you need to probe to find out specifics about these referrals and their business in order to create a powerful cover letter. Suppose your new referral is in a business in which you have never been before. You would then need to explain your accomplishments and articulate how those skills are easily transferable to other industries, in particular, the referral's (in whatever industry they are).

Be aggressive

When writing your letter, take the responsibility for being the one who is going to move this process along. Do not wait for or expect others to take initiative on your behalf. For example, in the cover letter, be specific as to the day and time you will call them back to inquire about the next step.

Also in your cover letter, you should let your audience know how much you want the job, or you are interested in working for their company. Don't be afraid to tell them how much and why you are interested in the opportunity. This is another way to separate you from the others. Companies and people like to hear that an applicant really wants to work for them. And most applicants fail to say it!

The following are some sample cover letters that work and a few that don't:

COVER LETTER 1 (DOES NOT WORK)

In this cover letter, Michael only speaks of himself, but never references the company to which he is writing, or how his prior experience could be an asset to the company. Michael uses general terms in describing what's important to him. If I were the recipient of this letter, I would be more interested in whether he knew what my business was about and if he had an idea of what's important to me. It is clear that this individual has not done any due diligence and has no idea what the company does.

The business experience mentioned, though impressive, does not demonstrate how it is transferable to the target audience's business, and what the benefit is to the company in having this individual on board. Basically Michael is saying, "I am great and if you give me a chance I will show you how I can do great things for you too."

How could this person really help when they have not even demonstrated an initial inkling that they know something about the target audience's business? This is a turn off. Don't make the same mistake.

Michael J. Merloni
310 Oneonta Way
Westfield, New Jersey 07090
Phone (908) 555-8723 Fax (908) 555-9852
merloni@home.com

September 24, 2001

John R. Darcy
President
CM Ltd.
95 Longwharf Rd.
Boston, MA 02116

Dear Mr. Darcy:

Could I help you as a regional General Manager or Senior Sales Executive based in the New York/ Philadelphia area?

I have been a national sales leader at Oracle, D&B and ADP. Most recently, I have led (as President) the turn around of a software division of CheckFree to record profits and customer satisfaction. Previously, I founded a nationally recognized mid-market ERP Systems Integration business.

I am far more interested in an intriguing business that requires the challenge of dynamic leadership. However, you should know that in recent years my total compensation has ranged from $315,000 to $500,000-plus.

If you need a proven executive to achieve the results you and your stakeholders expect, I believe I can help.

Sincerely,

Michael Merloni

COVER LETTER 2 (DOES WORK)

In this cover letter, you can see from the outset the tone is much different from Michael's letter. Malcolm personalized it and clearly demonstrated that he had done his homework. The way he introduced his knowledge of the industry referencing a recent press clipping was a nice touch. In addition, the Malcolm did an excellent job of demonstrating how his previous experience could help the company. The conclusion of the second paragraph where he stated, "We completed the project on time and under budget," subtly highlighted the real benefit of having him involved. Finally Malcolm did not let Ms. Burke "off the hook." He reminded her that they had agreed to speak at a specific day and time and he planned on calling at that time. If I was the hiring manager and received a cover letter such as this, I would want to talk to Malcom ASAP.

April 10, 2002

Ms. Lori Burke
President
XYZ Corporation
110 Redwood Drive
San Jose, CA 95101

Dear Lori;

Thank you for taking the time to speak with me earlier today. I just got off the phone with Christine and she asked me to send you her regards.

I appreciated your candor and the opportunity to forward my resume. My experience at Oracle has been very rewarding, but, as we discussed on the phone, I am ready for my next challenge. Your organization has received favorable press lately and I am very intrigued by your recent acquisition. I feel the combination of the two organizations will position your company well for the future. I believe I can help in the area of merging the two computer systems. I have participated in an initiative like this when we acquired EFG corporation. I was responsible for managing a team of 20, comprised of consultants, developers, and testers. My expertise in data mining allowed us to preserve critical customer information without having any down time. We completed the project on time and under budget.

As we discussed, I will follow up with you by phone next Tuesday to discuss my candidacy. I will call you at 11 a.m.

Thank you again for your consideration.

Respectfully,

Malcom Dakin

Cover Letter 3 (does work)

This cover letter also starts out very strong. Chris references the connection, introduces his experience, and lets Mark know up front why this is important. It is clear to me that Chris asked Jim, his contact, detailed questions to identify Mark's "hot buttons." Also it appears that Jim coached Mark on how best to get Mark's attention.

In the second paragraph, Chris let Mark know he has done his initial homework on the company, and was able to articulate his potential value to Mark's strategic growth. Here is where Mark can start to develop a mental picture of Chris.

In the third paragraph, Chris does a nice job of demonstrating what he is known for, how his expertise is transferable, and how he sees himself contributing to Mark's initiative. Notice how he was able to articulate his strengths as it fit with what is important to Mark.

So far, Chris has distinguished himself as a viable candidate. Knowing Jim certainly helped and gave him some credibility. But it was merely temporary. The facts are that Chris seized the opportunity by leveraging off the relationship with Jim to open the door, used Jim as a "coach" in the process to gain insight into the best way to make a favorable impression on Mark, did enough due diligence to get a good understanding of what Mark was looking for and what his "hot buttons," were and was able to articulate his value proposition in a way that should get a favorable response.

March 2, 2002

Mr. Mark Fallon
Chief Financial Officer
MFS Consulting
42 Post Road
Hartford, CT

Dear Mark;

Jim Peters suggested I forward my resume for your review based on the conversation you had with him earlier this week. My experience and background in managing Client Services in the professional services market. He said you might be looking to hire someone with my credentials.

From the due diligence I did on MFS I learned that you are about to embark on selling your CRM software to Financial Services companies. I think I can help. I believe, based on my experience working with Fleet, JP Morgan Chase, and Fidelity (to name a few), I can add value to your initiative.

I have been recognized in the past for my business development; strategic planning; and operational and marketing expertise. In my present capacity (with one of your biggest competitors) I am responsible for delivering 13 percent of our company's revenue and 20 percent of full year EBIT. Based on my conversations with Jim, it sounds as though this is exactly the type of growth you are looking for in your new business unit.

I would welcome the opportunity to meet with you to gain a better understanding of your current and future needs. I will call you on Thursday, March 7th to schedule an appointment when your schedule permits.

Respectfully,

Chris Stein

Resumes

You might already have a resume. You might think it's pretty good. It just might be, but it can't be the one you send out anymore. Like your cover letter, you need to customize this document, too. Whether you are developing your resume from scratch, or just doing some fine tuning by simply rearranging the information, you must prepare each one as it relates to your target audience's requirements.

Let's say you just got off the phone with a referral. You had a great conversation, and this person asked you to send your resume. As you reflect on the conversation, you'll realize that you now know more about this person and their company than you did prior to the call. Do you think your current resume, as constructed, will work? The answer is rarely, if ever, yes. You'll want to design your resume to be responsive to what was discussed during your conversation.

Your resume is a document that needs to pique someone's interest in the first 45 to 60 seconds. You *must* give them a compelling reason to continue to read and any information you know about the person or situation must be utilized to its fullest.

An excellent resume that someone will actually read must have the following three criteria:

1. **Customize.** From phone conversations and the due diligence you do on a person, industry, or company, you will gain some knowledge that can be communicated in your resume. For example, you learned during the phone conversation that the referral is looking for someone with sales management experience in their particular industry. You have both sales and marketing management experience. Your current resume deemphasizes

your sales management in any particular industry and accentuates your marketing expertise. You would not send the current resume as is. You would modify your current resume to play up your sales management experience and down play your marketing expertise. This would not require a major overhaul, just some fine-tuning to get your resume to be a tailored fit.

2. **Respond to hot buttons.** Your current resume probably has 80 to 90 percent generic information that could apply to most of the opportunities you are considering. The extra 10 to 20 percent difference is the fine-tuning you must do to respond to your target audience's hot buttons. That is what is going to allow your resume to clearly stand out from the others.

3. **Keep it simple.** You want your resume to be easy to read and flow. The best way to analyze that is to put yourself in the shoes of your target audience. Review both your cover letter and resume objectively (or with your mentor) and see if they would interest *you* if you were the hiring manager.

You want the resume to be action-oriented so people get excited about you. There are two things that need to be communicated in every statement you make about what you have done: the features and benefits of each statement. *Feature* is the distinguishing characteristic you want to emphasize.

Benefit is how someone did or will benefit from this feature. Here are a few examples:

Vice President of Marketing

Established programs to support expanding sales organization resulting in 50 percent of annual lead requirements generated in four months.

Feature: Established programs to support expanding sales organization

Benefit: resulting in 50 percent of annual lead requirements generated in four months.

Purchasing Manager

Negotiated and implemented a nationwide contract with an office supply vendor that resulted in annual cost reduction over $300,000 and service consistency.

Feature: Negotiated and implemented a nationwide contract with an office supply vendor

Benefit: that resulted in annual cost reduction over $300,000 and service consistency.

Human Resource Professional

Implemented selection and retention techniques that improved product and service quality.

Feature: Implemented selection and retention techniques

Benefit: that improved product and service quality.

Getting your target audience's attention immediately: the beginning

Now that you have an understanding of what should be in your resume, you need to start working on the structure.

The beginning of the resume is pivotal. This is where your target audience will formulate a mental picture of you professionally. Many people start out by having a statement about their objective. Don't bother. Most objective statements are bland and really do not say much about a person that distinguishes them. Usually they are something such as, "I want to work in an environment where there is an opportunity for growth." Who wants to work for a company where you can never get ahead? "I want to work for a company with smart people." Who wants to work for a company with dummies? In a document of such importance, you cannot afford to offer meaningless statements.

Whether you are in a senior or junior position, your departure point should be a Summary of Qualifications, or Profile. You want to provide your target audience with bullet points of things that really distinguish your experience and expertise.

Here are some sample bullet points that have been taken from strong resumes:

* Obtained $10 million in first round funding for technology startup and achieved $2.5 million in first year revenue.

* Transformed failing software company; sold for $18 million with 100-percent shareholder ROI.

* Drove 45-percent margin improvement by redesigning business model for $3 billion product division.

- ◆ Writer/producer of multimedia marketing and sales presentation projects for major Hollywood motion picture and television studios.

- ◆ Understanding of financial, operational, reimbursement, and utilization issues that impact healthcare delivery within a variety of healthcare organizations: HMO, hospitals, IPA.

Make sure you do not fall into the trap of including generalities that could be about anyone. These are the type of things you might think give someone insight into you, but in reality are generic comments which so many others. Here are some samples:

- ➤ Insightful and responsive manager with a proven record of success.

- ➤ Persistent problem solver.

- ➤ Thrives on challenges, excels under pressure, and always gets the job done.

- ➤ Team player.

- ➤ Possess excellent interpersonal and communication skills.

- ➤ Hands on.

- ➤ Persuasive negotiator dealing effectively across all levels of the organization.

- ➤ Accustomed to a fast pace and to working on multiple projects at once.

- ➤ Forward thinker.

- ➤ Results-oriented.

As you think of the things you want your target audience to know about you and before you list any of your bullet points, bear in mind *features and benefits*:

Keeping your target audience's attention: the main body

Now that your target audience is engaged in your resume, they are interested in learning more about your professional background. Here is where you describe the companies you have worked for, when you were there, what your responsibilities were, and what you did that made a difference. The headers for this section would generally be either Work History or Business Experience. Here are two examples:

Experience

E-Parcel, Division of Mitsubishi Electronics of America, Newton, MA   **1997—Present**

Start-up venture focused on advanced file delivery technology and desktop management software over the Internet.

Director of Sales—Managed and directed team of 15 account executives selling to Fortune 500 companies. Responsible for creating compensation and incentive plans, recruiting and training, and developing sales strategy for the entire product line.

Accomplishments

- Grew sales to $3 million in 1st year with a 20-percent net profit.
- Developed non-traditional customer renewal program resulting in 100-percent retention.
- Surpassed revenue projections every year by average of 125 percent by providing cutting-edge products guaranteeing a competitive edge for clients.

**3/94–4/99   Twentieth Century Fox Film Corporation
Los Angeles, CA**

Motion picture and television production company.

Manager, Multimedia Presentations
Reported to the President of Fox Licensing. Responsible for the writing, design, and production of Fox's multimedia presentations to retailers, licensees, corporate partners, and film exhibitors.

* Developed X-Files Website, which receives 150,000 visits per day and achieved 37-percent net return on merchandise sales.

* Created business model being used for selling Fox entertainment merchandise via the Internet which is still in use and which generated in excess of $5 million in the first year.

* Recognized for developing innovative programs that are now being used for additional Fox film projects such as *King of the Hill* and *Planet Ice*.

You want to make sure you list any relevant experiences you have had. If you have done other things in your life that are not particularly relevant to the job you are pursuing, a quick line will suffice, listing:

➤ The company.

➤ Dates of employment.

➤ Title and responsibilities.

You do not have to do more than that. If people are interested, they will ask. You want your resume to be succinct and straight to the point about what is relevant to your target audience. Any more is a waste of space and time.

Wrapping up your resume: closing remarks

Here is where you will list your education and any training you have that is relevant, such as certifications. You do not need to start listing all the training classes you have taken in your career. Just relate facts that are distinguishing and that specifically relate to what might be important to your target audience.

There is no need to mention things such as hobbies, personal information, or references. It really has no bearing on what you are trying to accomplish, is old school, and 95 percent of your competition mindlessly puts it in theirs.

Resumes That Do Work

You want your resume to have a nice flow. Here are the characteristics that make a resume stand out from the crowd:

➤ **Easy to read and easy to follow.** Bullet points are easy to follow. Your audience can easily go through an initial look within 45 to 60 seconds. After that, they *want* to read more or take more time to evaluate your candidacy.

➤ **Results oriented.** You want to send a strong message that you are successful and outstanding in your field, creating a clear mental picture of who you are, and what you "bring to the table."

➤ **Use of action oriented words.** Use words such as: developed, established, created, managed, installed, planned, pro-actively identified, researched, conceived, successfully delivered, led a team, grew, co-developed, supported, and managed. These are all powerful ways to make a favorable impression. They give your target audience an excellent understanding of what you have done and of what you are potentially capable.

➤ **Engaging.** You want your resume to leave your audience feeling that they want to learn more about you and would look forward to speaking with you.

Resumes That Don't Work

Limit your resume to a length of two pages. You are using your resume to position yourself for an interview and to pique a potential employers interest. A resume that is way too long and written like a novel is hard on the eyes written is and difficult to understand. Verbiage used to describe your responsibilities will be buried in content. There will be a lot of great stuff about you that no one will read. I seriously doubt your target audience is going to take the time to read a resume that looks like a novel. It's just too much work. Do you think anyone can get through a first glance in 45 to 60 seconds? Obviously, the answer is no.

If you pull a resume format from the Internet, your target audience can spot this quickly and determine it is broad based, very canned, and really doesn't not say much about you and how your experience relates to the their business.

If you follow the advice given in this chapter, you will find that your cover letters and resumes will get a favorable response. People will actually compliment you because you will have responded to what your target audience thinks is important. Your referral or contact will perceive you as "a person that gets it." Now they will go out of their way to let the "right person" know you are someone they should meet.

Award-winning Performance:

Prepare for the Interview

"**D**o you have some time to talk to another person? We'd like you to meet José, our warehouse manager." Sheila smiled and replied, "Sure, I have the time." She arrived at this plumbing supply company almost three hours ago for a one-hour interview—but it turned into a real "meet the family" scenario. It had started with Roy, the owner. She had been warned that Roy "lived and breathed" the business, so Sheila had boned up on plumbing supplies ahead of time—and he was obviously impressed. Roy introduced her to Joyce, the current office manager. Joyce asked some nitty-gritty questions about how she would recruit and retain the office staff. Sheila described how she had handled that issue at her last employer, and they really hit it off. By the end of their long talk, Joyce made it clear that she thought Sheila was perfect for the job and took Sheila around to meet the office workers, the three salesmen, and the controller.

Now it looked as if they weren't going to let her go home until she met everyone in the company.

All this networking stuff has a pay-off. The phone calls, cover letters, and resumes you send will open doors. You will have interviews scheduled. Now we will focus on the interview so you will be able to make it easy for the company to see that you are the right person for them. Your understanding or insight into the company, the way you ask and respond to questions, and how you dress all have an impact on how well the interview goes.

The interview is not only about evaluating your ability, but it is about assessing your interpersonal chemistry and fit with an organization. Hiring managers are significantly swayed by personality. If your technical skills and other factors are even close to an organization's requirements, the person who has the most compatible personality will get the job every time.

Determining Chemistry and Fit

The interviewing process allows a company to assess your skills, background, intelligence, and growth potential. The fact that you are already at the interview probably means that they believe you have the right background. The interviewer's goal is to understand your personality, energy level, interaction, and conversational style.

Not only is the organization assessing how you fit during the interview process, but you should be assessing how *they* fit with *you*! Don't lose sight of the fact that you must be analyzing the situation just as much as they are. There is a tendency for people to feel the company has the upper hand in the interview because they have the job and you are trying to get it. Remember that, in order for this to work, it must be good for both sides, and in that sense you are equal partners. Think about whether you could work for this person or could fit in with the organization.

At one time in my career I took a position where the chemistry was not great and it did not feel like a fit for me. It was a disaster. I was accustomed to working for organizations that were considered best in their class. This particular company did not have a great reputation and was considered to be average at best. I thought I could fix it. I was wrong. I ended up leaving sooner than planned. Do not make the same mistake. You'll be miserable the whole time. If your instincts tell you to stay away, listen to them.

Just because a company wants you it does not mean you have to pursue the opportunity. Make sure that during the interview process you constantly assess the situation and that it feels good to you. Make sure the chemistry is there, in particular with the person to whom you will be reporting.

Getting Ready to Make a Good Impression

The structure of an interview will vary depending on who in the organization you will be meeting. You need to find out who is going to be participating in the interview process. This information should not be difficult to attain because in order to set up the interview, you obviously have corresponded with someone from the company. Don't hesitate to ask what your schedule is going to be because you need to budget the appropriate time in your day. Once you know the time frame, it should be comfortable to ask for the names and titles of the people you will be meeting.

Crib Sheet (if you need it)

If you have already done your due diligence on a company or person (by following the guidelines in Chapter 3), read the material over again before you go in for an interview. If you have not done the work, now is the time.

Some people are nervous about the interview process and feel like they need some quick reminders before they walk into an interview. It's okay to prepare a crib sheet that you could slip into your pocket and refer to. Use it to review your main points before you go into the interview. You may look at them while you are waiting in the reception area or in your car. However, *do not take it out during the interview*!

Here's a good example of an effective crib sheet:

COMPANY:	TCD.
BACKGROUND:	3rd largest privately held staffing firm in USA, $60 plus million in annual revenue. Been in business 24 years.
DISTINGUISHING CHARACTERISTICS:	Offers 100-percent money back service guarantee, nationwide service capability through centralized location, aligned by industry, well-respected senior management team, and excellent reputation.
COMPETITORS:	Aquent, CDI, Adecco.
HOT BUTTONS:	Loyalty, perseverance, and work ethic.
POINTS TO MAKE:	My prior industry experience, network of contacts, and I want the job.
QUESTIONS TO ASK:	What are the company's greatest challenges these days? How will you measure my progress and success?

Hiring managers generally solicit the opinion of the other people involved in the interview process, so the impression you make on all of them will determine whether the hard work you've done to get to this point will pay off.

Know Your Target Audience

It's important to understand who your target audience is in order to be effective when the interview begins. Every person you are going to meet has a unique personality and role within an organization. Similarly, each has a different role during the interview process.

➤ **The big cheese.** This person could be the CEO, COO, CFO or similarly-titled member of the senior management team. This person understands the total organization, how it comes together, and should have a vision for the future. The big cheese will ask you questions and want very direct answers. Do not ramble with this person. Be very succinct. Everything is all about how you can contribute to the bottom line.

➤ **Your boss.** This is the person to whom you will be reporting directly. The boss wants to know in detail how you can help make life easier or better. This person really wants to know how you do things and what makes you tick. At this level, you want to be specific about how you get things done.

➤ **Human resources.** These people will have a bearing on the interview process but probably not as much influence as the Big Cheese and Boss. Do not, however, under estimate their influence.

They'll speak to you about the company, culture, and benefits. They'll be assessing whether you fit in.

➤ **Coach.** This person could be the referral, contact, or someone you've identified who can give you good information about the company and the people wiht whom you are interviewing. This person can help you identify what the company is looking for, tell you what to be careful about, and —depending on the situation—know about your competition. The coach might even have the ability to help influence the decision and put a good word in for you. Stay in touch with this person throughout the entire process with this specific company.

Dress for the Interview

You have an opportunity to really impress your target audience with your appearance. Do not overdo it. Dress in a manner that is appropriate for the environment. You do not want to distract the interviewer with what you are wearing. You want to keep them focused on you and what you have to say.

First impressions are long lasting. Dressing like a professional means:

➤ Dark suit (not a sport coat).

➤ White shirt (men), white blouse (women).

➤ Dark belt, no flashy buckle (unless you're interviewing in Texas).

➤ Blue or red tie (men).

➤ Black, shined shoes. (No boots, even if they are Ferragamos you bought in Italy last year!)

Interview Do's

Here are some pointers to remember before you walk in for the interview:

✓ **Relax.** Take a few deep breaths. If you are nervous, you will have trouble listening and reacting at your best. You may have trouble articulating what it is you want this person to know about you. Slow yourself down. The best way to get over your anxiety is to block everything out and just concentrate on what is being said.

✓ **Mirror the body tempo.** Take the lead from the interviewer. Whether the interviewer is laid back, or a Type A personality, react accordingly. Always sit up in your chair, leaning forward intently.

✓ **Observe office surroundings.** Look at the decor (desk, walls, bookcase) and figure out what type of interests the interviewer has. Is the interviewer a golfer, animal lover, or family oriented?

✓ **Break the ice based on observation.** This is a great way to get the conversation started and spend a minute attempting to develop a personal connection with the interviewer. You may find common business ground and spend a significant part of the interview discussing these things. That's okay if it happens. It is probably a sign that the interviewer is starting to assess how you would fit in the organization.

✓ **Have a positive attitude.** Being around positive people is contagious. It is a great way to make a positive impression. Recruiters and hiring managers have told me the single most distinguishing characteristic that separates candidates is attitude. Positive people get hired. People who want to gripe about their last boss do not.

✓ **Arrive 15 minutes early.** Not only will it ensure that you're there on time, it also will give you an opportunity to observe the culture and pace of the environment. Do people look happy? Are they friendly with each other? It should give you a good idea of what it would be like to work there.

✓ **Bring a note pad and pens.** The interviewer is going to make some points you will probably want to reference during your response. It may be in five minutes or an hour later. This way you have the information at your fingertips. It sends a strong message to the interviewer that you are there to conduct business and listen to what is being said.

✓ **Ask for permission to take notes.** This shows respect for the interviewer and process. One caution: Be discreet when taking the notes. First of all, don't take too many or you'll look like a secretary. Hit the highlights only and jot down key words while maintaining decent eye contact with your interviewer.

Interview Don'ts

Here a few things you definitely do not want to do. Some of it may appear to be common sense, but I can assure you people do these things all the time and never get asked back:

×   **Don't take off your suit jacket.** I don't care how hot it gets. You are in a formal meeting. Treat it that way.

×   **Don't exaggerate or fabricate your ability.** Be comfortable with who you are. If you are asked a question and feel tempted to embellish, don't. You will likely come across as insincere, creating an uncomfortable situation. Most importantly, why try to attain a job under false pretenses? Eventually it will catch up to you. You'd be surprised how much people will respect you for being forthright. Do the right thing.

×   **Don't put your feet, elbows, or anything else on the interviewer's desk.** You might be laughing at this, but I can tell you from experience that while elbows are more common, there are even a few people who have violated their interviewer's space with their feet. This mostly happens when candidates think they are doing great—they let their guard down and put their feet up.

×   **Don't drink soda or coffee (even if it is offered).** Water is acceptable. If you spill coffee or soda it could become a real mess and change the whole mood. I visited an office once where a candidate spilled coffee on the owner's oriental rug. The owner was so upset he could not concentrate during the interview.

×   **Don't chew gum.** It is impolite and unprofessional.

Questions

The ability to not only answer questions well but to be able to ask intelligent, relevant, and interesting questions will leave a lasting impression on your target audience. It requires discipline, focus, and an ability to pay attention to what is being said.

Answering questions

You must be a good listener at all times. You may be asked questions relevant to points discussed earlier in the interview. If you have not been listening well, you will now be defensive.

The biggest and most common mistake people make in an interview is to tune out interviewers while they are still speaking because they are formulating their next response. Thinking of what you want to say and continuing to listen are not mutually exclusive events—you can and must do them both simultaneously. Practice this awareness in everyday life and you will notice that every once in a while someone is talking to you, you realize you have no idea what was said during the last 30 seconds because your mind was wandering. This can really hurt you in the interview setting.

If you are not clear about how to respond to a question do not hesitate to ask for clarification. Here are some pointers on how to make a favorable impression when answering questions:

> ➤ **Demonstrate strong listening skills by pausing in-between the question asked and the answer you give.** You are not in a race. Pausing will give you a few extra seconds to get your thoughts together. It also sends a subliminal message that you are a good listener.

➤ **If it's a long-winded statement that precedes the question or you are not sure how to answer, have the interviewer repeat the question or put it into different words.** For example you may say something such as, "Let me make sure I understand what you're looking for (or what you meant). You want to know about project lead, not project management, experience?"

➤ **Your answers need to be clear and spoken with confidence and conviction.** Keep your energy high, but controlled. Let people feel your passion and excitement.

➤ **When possible, use specific examples to demonstrate your experience and capabilities when responding to questions.** Your interviewer wants to hire someone who can help the company. Making it clear that you can perform, and have performed well in the past will help your cause. The strength of your examples will have a major influence on the interviewer gaining confidence in your ability. Have your stories ready. Practice telling them. Keep your stories short and to the point.

➤ **Use features, benefits, and proof sources when referencing examples.** The feature would be what you did. Key words in this spirit are made, saved, or achieved. The benefit is what it meant to your former company (or could mean to their company if you did the same thing for them). The proof source would be giving a real life example by describing the actual company or project.

Asking questions

There are two reasons that you ask questions. The obvious reason is to get responses, which you digest and the cumulative information helps you evaluate the opportunity. Just as important, however, is that you need to ask intelligent, insightful questions to make yourself look good in the eyes of the interviewer. This is an outstanding opportunity to distinguish yourself from your competition. Imagine if there are three job finalists and when asked if they have any questions, two of them respond, "No you've covered everything," but the third says, "I was wondering if you could give me your perspective on how morale is in your department." It's obvious who looks better.

I also strongly suggest that when meeting more than one person during the process (which is almost always the case), pick one or two critical questions and ask each of the interviewers the exact same question. The answers you receive will provide you with real insight into the company. If there is consistency in the answers, that is generally a good thing. If not, you may need to investigate further. Here is a list, in no particular order, of good questions that cover most of what you need to evaluate an opportunity. Do not feel obligated to ask them all:

- ➤ What makes this a good for which company to work?

- ➤ What are the company's greatest challenges at this time?

- ➤ Could you describe the role model in your company or department who is highly successful?

- ➤ What are the distinguishing characteristics that make people think so highly of this person?

➤ What processes do you utilize that make your company (or department) unique?

➤ What would I have to do to be successful in your company (or department)?

➤ If you were me and you started in this position tomorrow, what would you do first to make an impact on the company (or department)?

➤ What is your management style?

➤ How is the morale in your department specifically and in the company overall?

➤ How will I know if I am meeting or exceeding your expectations?

➤ How will you measure my progress and success?

➤ Why is this position available?

➤ Where did the incumbent fall short? (If appropriate.)

➤ Do you have any other candidates?

➤ How do I stack up against the others?

The Call-Back Interview

If you follow the advice you've received so far, you will more than likely advance to the next phase of the interview process: the call back. It's great that they asked you back, but do not get overconfident. You still do not have the job. You have more selling to do.

Just as you did prior to earlier interviews, you want to get as much information as possible about the next round. And because they obviously like you and are bringing you back, you should have no problem getting the answers to the following questions:

- ➤ Who will I be meeting with?
- ➤ What will they want to discuss?
- ➤ How much time will I have with each person?
- ➤ Can you tell me a little about each person's professional background and personality?
- ➤ How many other people are under consideration for this position?
- ➤ Where do I stack up?
- ➤ If things go well in this next interview, what happens next?

You also want to contact your insider "coach" (if you have one). They will be able to give you the scoop about what's really going on, how you came off, where you stand in the process, insight into the people you will be interviewing with, and any other relevant information that can give you a competitive edge.

You must get answers to these questions so you can once again prepare intelligent questions and do more due diligence on the people you will be meeting. Most people just "wing" these interviews because they feel good about getting asked back. Your careful preparation is another way you will separate yourself from the pack.

Final Interview Preparation

Your call-back interviews went well. Now you're down to the last round. At this stage of the process, you need to differentiate yourself from the other final candidates and demonstrate to the company that *you* are the best person for the job.

It's pretty obvious that you are a serious candidate, but just because you are invited for a final interview does not mean it is a "slam dunk." Even if there is only one other candidate, your odds are still less than 50/50 because the options the company has also include delaying the process, not hiring someone at all, or entertaining last-second applicants. As the old Smith Barney commercials used to say, you are going to have to earn it."

Before you go in for the final interview, here is what you need to do:

➤ Contact the person setting up the final interview and go through the same type of questions you did before the last round of interviews.

➤ Contact your coach for the same reasons.

➤ Do some additional due diligence and do not take anything for granted. You've already spent a great deal of time at the company and surely there are issues and details which have come up that you can research further.

➤ Have your references ready! Call the people you're using as a reference and prepare them. Tell them you are at the final interview stage and ask for permission to use them as a reference. It's important that you give them some detail about what the job is, how they can support you best when giving the reference (by now you know what the company considers critical), and how important it is that they help you with the reference because you *really* want this job.

➤ Don't e-mail your references to the company! Give them to the interviewer in person as soon as they ask. It is preferable to give the names and phone numbers of your references off the top of your head. This shows a measure of skill as opposed to handing them a sheet with names and numbers on it. It's subtle, but helpful. If that creates a problem for you, the printed sheet will do.

One final note. This may be the final interview but *don't forget the basics.* Dress appropriately, be on time, and have particularly good questions ready. These things are just as important now, if not more so, than they were before your first session. Many people back down at this point because they feel they're gaining control of things. This is not the case. You gain a measure of control when you have an offer in your hand, and not a moment before.

If you follow the interview guidelines detailed in this chapter, you will be able to walk into any situation with a high degree of confidence. You think you are ready for an interview? Before you say yes, you must answer each question correctly. This time it's a true/false exam.

True   False

☐   ☐   1. The interview is not only about evaluating your ability, but also about assessing your interpersonal chemistry and fit with an organization.

☐   ☐   2. During the interview, the person to whom you will be reporting wants to know how you can make life easier or better and wants you to be specific about how you get things accomplished.

☐   ☐   3. The single most distinguishing characteristic that separates candidates is attitude.

☐ ☐ 4. It is okay to accept a glass of water if it is offered, but you should not accept coffee or soda when offered.

☐ ☐ 5. When providing answers to questions, you should use features, benefits, and proof sources when referencing examples.

☐ ☐ 6. If you meet with more than one person during the process, you should have one or two questions and ask each of the interviewers the exact same question.

☐ ☐ 7. It is helpful to have a "coach" in the process to provide insight into a company which may give you a distinct competitive advantage.

If you answered true to all of the statements, you are going to do extremely well on your interviews and will be ready to start evaluating offers.

Expert Strategies:

Negotiate Your Best Deal

J eff tapped at the keys, filling in the columns on his computer screen, and frowned in concentration. He had just landed not one, but two job offers, and he was faced with a dilemma he could only have dreamed of when he was laid off a month ago—which job to take. Both salaries were respectable, about what he was making before, and in this market, that was an accomplishment in itself. No one else on his team had even one offer yet. So should he risk trying to negotiate further? Or should he just accept one of the offers—and if so, which one?

He sat back and stared at the results of his efforts: He had created a grid of two tables including three columns headed Needs, Wants, and Wishes. "Hmm, interesting—the offer from Infotek covers all of my needs and a few of my wants. The one from CIS has all my wants and few of my needs. I hadn't realized that before I laid it out this way. In reality, that pretty much narrows it down to Infotek. The only question now is whether to accept their offer as is, or try to negotiate the terms. What should my negotiating points be?"

When all the interviewing is over and the company is interested in you, you are entering the critical decision making period. When you receive an offer, or offers, you need to stay calm. There can be a lot of emotional ups and downs. Be ready for an emotional roller coaster.

Any serious offer will not be just about money. You need to look at what the *entire* offer represents, including things such as job environment, the long-range opportunity, your role and responsibility, the company's viability (particularly in a recessionary period), and the chemistry you developed during the interview process. After you evaluate the opportunity on those merits, you will be in a position to determine what you are willing to negotiate. If you have performed as described in previous chapters and can execute everything you will learn in this chapter, you will be able to negotiate from a position of strength.

Negotiating the Package

It's a good feeling when a company really wants you. You must be confident in your ability to negotiate a good deal. Lots of people fail at negotiating because they lack self-confidence, are afraid to ask, or just simply feel they are without power. They might be afraid of offending the person making the offer by asking for more. The fact is that if you negotiate in good faith and handle yourself professionally, negotiation is a common and well-accepted part of the hiring process.

There is no guarantee you will receive what you ask for, but you'll never get what you don't ask for.

In most negotiations, both sides are reasonable and somebody, or everybody, compromises a little to come to agreement. Do not be greedy, but do not sell yourself short. You want to put pen to paper and create a decision tree. This will help you evaluate your options so you can conduct the negotiation process in a non-emotional and rational way, which will lead to either success, or to you making a rational decision that this company is not for you.

Step 1: Developing your list of negotiating points—Your Needs, Wants, and Wishes

The foundation of your decision tree starts with your ability to divide your goals into three categories: needs, wants, and wishes. These three things form the basis for your negotiations. These goals should be used as your reference guide to determine whether an offer meets your requirements during the different stages of the negotiation process.

- **Needs.** These are the things you *must* have, such as salary, health benefits, and vacation time.

- **Wants.** These are things you would really *like* to have. They are the types of things you visualize for yourself in a particular environment that you *want* to have. These include things such as a bonus structure, a car, a 401(k) plan, additional vacation time, tuition reimbursement, or an expense account. These are things you deem important, but if you don't get all of them, it will not be the end of the world.

➤ **Wishes.** These are pie-in-the-sky things you *wish* for in an ideal situation. These types of things would be: membership to a fitness, golf, or tennis club, first class travel for all international flights, guaranteed bonus, or signing bonus. If you get any of these, you will be ecstatic, but you probably won't, and you need to evaluate any rejected requests here in the context of how you do with your needs and wants.

When you mix your needs, wants, and wishes together, you probably will not get everything you are asking for. However, it should lead you to a fair compromise, which is what negotiating is all about.

Here's an example:

Needs:

➤ At least $100,000 salary.

➤ 70-percent medical benefit coverage.

➤ Two weeks vacation.

Wants:

➤ $115,000 salary.

➤ 100-percent family medical coverage.

➤ Four weeks vacation.

➤ Car or monthly car allowance.

➤ 100-percent tuition reimbursement.

➤ Performance based bonus.

➤ 401(k) plan.

➤ Health club membership.

Wishes:

- ➤ Golf membership.

- ➤ Signing bonus of $10,000.

- ➤ Guaranteed first year bonus of at least 25 percent of salary.

- ➤ Life Insurance.

- ➤ 401(k) company match.

- ➤ Short-term and long-term disability insurance.

Based on this example, you may not get the golf membership, but you might get the health club membership. You may not get everything you request, but you will probably get some of them. Just make sure it is reasonable.

Create a general list to work from. (See page 206.) It will likely change slightly depending on the particular company and opportunity you pursue, but at least you will have a head start when you get to that juncture.

Step 2: Evaluating the offer

The next phase of the decision tree is considering the offer. Every offer situation is different. However, there are some basic components that must be defined in any offer that is made to you:

- ➤ The opportunity.

- ➤ Title.

- ➤ Role and responsibility.

- ➤ Salary.

- ➤ Benefits.

- ➤ Travel.

NEEDS, WANTS, AND WISHES WORKSHEET

Needs	Wants	Wishes

The other things you won't see in an offer letter, but you should evaluate when considering an offer are:

- **The company's viability.** Are they solid financially? The last thing you want to do is join a sinking ship.

- **The people.** During the week, you spend more waking hours with people at work than you do with your family. The single greatest factor in your day-to-day enjoyment (or lack thereof) at work will be the people surrounding you.

- **Environment.** Is this the type of place that fits well with your personality? You want to make sure this place "feels right" to you.

- **The company's value proposition.** Do you believe in what they are doing? You must be fired up about where you work and the type of things the company does.

- **Company's reputation.** What are people saying? Once you sign the offer letter, you will be part of them. Make sure this is a place you can be proud to call yours.

- **Industry.** Is this where you want to be?

When analyzing these factors, it is essential that you be extremely honest with yourself. Base your analysis on what you saw and felt, not on what you are hoping for. There can be a natural temptation to look for the positives and ignore the negatives when you are looking to make a change. If you met people whom you were uncomfortable with, you cannot blindly hope that they will be totally different if you end up working there. Similarly, if you've picked up on things during the interviews that concerned you, do not ignore them.

They must be weighed. No place is perfect and you can be forgiving if the good outweighs the bad. But you can't afford to be in denial.

The fact that you are at this juncture is great. However, do not think for a minute you are home free.

Step 3: Compare the offer you have against your needs, wants, and wshes lists.

There can be a lot of stress, concern, panic, and miscommunication during negotiations. You are at a crossroad in your life and you can be emotionally vulnerable. Despite that, you need to keep an even keel and a clear head in order to properly evaluate the offer and get the best deal for yourself.

Offer Rules of Thumb

Here are some guidelines to consider which will help you close the deal:

▷ **Stay focused on the objective.** Landing a job is it. Do not let your pride, ego, and anything else get in the way.

▷ **Don't take anything personally or as an insult.** Sometimes things that are said, or *how* they are said in negotiations can be taken out of context or be misinterpreted. Do not let your emotions get in the way of making an intelligent decision.

▷ **Do not fixate on money.** Listen to the entire offer. There are so many different components of the package that you must evaluate it as a whole.

▷ **It is hard to negotiate for yourself.** Most employers know this, too. Don't be afraid to speak up.

▷ **Appear calm, even if you're not.** Do not appear desperate, overanxious, or ungrateful no matter how you feel inside or what the offer is. Be cool and professional.

▷ **It is perfectly fine to accept the offer on the spot if it is the job you want.** Some people feel you must ask for time to make a decision regardless of the circumstance. This is absolutely untrue. If you honestly need time to make a decision, politely ask when they need an answer by. Only ask for the additional time if driven by a real situation, such as legitimately not knowing if you want the job or if you want to wrap up other situations. If, however, you want the job and everything is acceptable, looking them right in the eye, accepting the job, and telling them how excited you are to join their company starts this new relationship off with some great momentum. Remember: Until a job is accepted, the company still has the right to rescind the offer. I have seen my share of people who kept their options open too long and suddenly an unexpected company-wide hiring freeze devastated this nonsensical game plan.

▷ **The offer is not exactly what you want, feel out the negotiator and find any elements which might get you closer to a deal:**

➤ What short-term and long-term plans does the company have for me?

➤ Are there any other benefits that we did not cover yet?

➤ Is there anything else I should know about the offer we did not cover?

➤ Is this the company's best offer, or are there any soft spots we could discuss?

You will need to look hard at your Needs, Wants, and Wish list when contemplating whether it is the right deal for you.

▷ **If the offer is low and you've identified money as an important issue,** you need to be prepared to respond immediately. Here is the type of response you should consider:

"Thank you very much for your offer. I appreciate your consideration. Is this the company's best offer or is this something that can be discussed further?"

➤ **If the response is yes,** be prepared and committed to say yes to them if the amended dollar amount is close to what you want. For example, let's say the original offer to you is $85,000 and this is your final item of concern. If you ask for $90,000, you must absolutely be prepared to accept the job if they honor your request. If you weren't prepared to do so you should have never have asked. Of course, if money is only one part of the negotiation, you are not as bound to a positive response because it depends on those other factors.

➤ **If the response is no,** thank them again and let them know you will get back to them with your answer.

➤ **If you get the question, "What will it take to get you?"** This is a common question and they are obviously referring to the salary component of the package. This common question is a great opportunity to provide them with your needs, wants, and wish list in the context of also stressing the importance of other non-financial issues. You get to show them you're not interested only in money.

Step 4: Outcome Decision Tool—Getting to win-win

The last part of your negotiation process decision tree is determining how to reach the right conclusion. You want to make sure you land in the right place for the right reasons.

The four likely negotiation scenarios that will occur are win-win, win-lose, lose-win, and lose-lose. Here is a little insight as to what is happening in each and what you should consider before you move forward:

- ➤ **Win-win.** Everyone gives a little, if at all, and is happy with the outcome. It happens occasionally that everything flows smoothly and all or most of the process simply comes together nicely. You might not have gotten everything from your wants and wish list, but it looks and feels like a great opportunity. Take the job.

- ➤ **Win-lose.** The negotiations were difficult. You feel as though you are compromising too much. They think it's a great deal, but your gut feelings tell you different. Think long and hard before you decide.

- ➤ **Lose-win.** You have asked for your needs and some wants but the company is complaining the whole way. You might find yourself getting angry. They are making you feel badly about what you are asking for. At the eleventh hour, they give in to your demands but not in a nice way. Things are unlikely to work out under this scenario. If this is the way things are at the honeymoon stage, what are the chances of a long-term marriage? You need to be very confident that bad feelings won't continue before you take this position.

➤ **Lose-lose.** Both parties are trying to make it work, but you can't come to terms. They propose you, "just start at these terms and after 90 days if you are as good as you say you are, we'll give you what you want." You're feeling as though this is an up-hill battle and the company has doubts you were not able to clear up during the interview process. Never take this job.

Negotiations are usually indicative of the way a person or company does business. If you were treated well in the process, chances are you will be happy working there. If you do not like the process, those chances are greatly reduced.

Going through the decision making tree process will enable you to evaluate all the critical factors you need to consider in order to make an informed decision. Because you have been doing such a good job paying attention this chapter, and if you got all the other quiz questions correct, we'll skip the chapter-ending quiz. You've earned the break. Just remember:

1. Create a list of needs, wants, and wishes as a basis for negotiations.

2. Develop and categorize a reasonable list of negotiating points.

3. Use the rule of thumb guide to help close the deal.

4. Don't be greedy. Focus on win-win.

By following the *SuperNetworking* system to this point, you have already put yourself in the top 5 percentile of people looking for a job.

Future Access:

Create a Network for Life

Ellen looked up from the file drawer in her home office and grabbed the next folder from the pile she was organizing. She realized it was all the networking contacts she had accumulated during her job search. In the excitement of starting her new job at the newspaper, she had been so busy the past few months that she hadn't even thought about her network. But as she flipped through the file folder, she suddenly stopped cold. "Hey! I forgot that Bill Goldstein was in here—he'd be a perfect source for that public utilities story I'm working on. How could I have forgotten that? And Ann Jones! I have to stay in touch with her. She knows everyone in media. Plus, I've got several names I should add to the database from my new job. I have to update this and get in touch with some of these people this week. My network is a gold mine!"

You've made it. The time and effort you've put forth in following this program has paid off. When you started out, you were not quite sure if you had it in you to stay the course, but you did, and now you realize just how much better off you are. You now have changed your life. Here's what you've done:

➤ Learned how to determine your value proposition and developed an effective elevator pitch that is narrowly focused and captures your target audience's attention, providing them with precisely what they need to know in order to help you.

➤ Organized and categorized your network of contacts appropriately.

➤ Learned how to "peel the onion" until you get to the core—to the right person that can help you.

➤ Learned the value of preparing for each phone call to make a favorable impression on everyone you speak with.

➤ Learned the importance of having a call strategy and objective, ensuring you reach your desired outcome for every conversation you have.

➤ Developed effective scripts that make it easy to ask for people to help.

➤ Learned how to find and use a mentor who was able to help you formalize the process and monitored your progress until you have landed your new job. You may need a mentor in the future. You are also now ready to mentor someone else.

➤ Learned how to prepare a weekly performance report that your mentor was able to use to hold you accountable.

➤ Developed customized cover letters and resumes that were unique and helped you separate yourself from the competition. Now you can use those writing skills to help you succeed with other projects.

➤ Learned how to prepare properly for interviews in order to make a favorable impression.

➤ Developed a decision tree to help you negotiate from strength and evaluate offers so you can feel confident throughout the process.

The Art of SuperNetworking

Attaining a job was just a by-product of the work you did and the new skills you developed. The art of SuperNetworking is a life skill that will change the way you function in the world. You are now better equipped to handle many challenges as your world continues to change. SuperNetworking is about building relationships—for life.

It is important to keep your network fresh and up-to-date throughout your life. If you do, you will be able to accomplish anything you want professionally or personally. Your life will become much easier.

What do you think will happen if you don't maintain your network? Think about the difference between you and someone else whose network is larger and stronger. Their ability to access people or information at a moment's notice allows them to be more efficient and effective than you. Think of the time saved by knowing how to get results quickly because you've made valuable connections for life.

I suppose you can think of the following story as an example of "practicing what I preach." When I decided to write this book, I felt there might be a business opportunity too. I wanted to create a networking methodology company and teach people in a workshop the same skills that you have developed from this book. I wanted to develop course curricula that could be delivered in a classroom environment. At the time, I really did not know much about the training business. My instincts told me to look at my network of contacts and see who would be able to help. My first call went to a contact, David a friend that used to work for a technical training organization. He liked my idea and put me in touch with his friend, Beran, who had written and published technical training manuals and was experienced in developing and selling workshops. Beran's insight into the business was invaluable. It helped shape my business plan. We had numerous dinners and lunches over the course of the next six months and he wanted nothing in return. He just wanted to help.

Beran contributed significantly to the launching of my company. He referred me to a great graphic designer who developed my brochure. As my network expanded, I was introduced to Rachel, an extremely talented Web designer who created *www.salmonsays.com*, and to Stacy, one of the country's top instructional designers who edited my workshop material. I am grateful for the opportunity to work with these people and I could never have accomplished these tasks without doing my own *SuperNetworking*.

By accessing my network of contacts, I was able to meet some very talented people who are now in my database permanently. I now know where to go when I need help in specific areas. This saves me a tremendous amount of time. In addition, these contacts, who were originally referrals, have introduced me to other people who have also helped contribute to the growth of my company. As an example, my graphic designer introduced me to a great printer.

Besides having a professional relationship with some of these people, a personal relationship has developed too. I play tennis with Beran and socialize with my graphic designer. They have each referred new clients to me over the course of time, and I have done the same for them. I attribute my successful relationships to the amount of time I put into developing and maintaining my network of contacts. That is the payoff of having a strong SuperNetwork. You just have to make it a priority. Don't wait until it's too late. Get in the habit now.

Giving and Receiving Is a Two-way Street

At the beginning of this process, you were the beneficiary of help from others. Once you get the job you want, it's important not to forget what others have done to help you get there. You are now in a position to return the favor and help others if and when they are doing their own networking. You are now going to be the one giving advice or allowing others to use your name to open up a door. You have an opportunity to be known as a resource, a Center of Influence (COI). This is someone that has the reputation of being well connected, a go-to person when someone needs something done. If you are always asking and never giving back, your network will be weak. You will be viewed as a "taker," not a "giver." Do not let this happen to you.

As Beran was helping me, I asked many times what I could do for him. I wanted to show my appreciation for all he had done for me. He said, "I just want to see you become successful and help in any way I can. Maybe you'll get the opportunity to help me in the future." Beran understands how a network should work.

I call Beran on a regular basis to stay in touch and to see how he is doing. We both get the opportunity to let each other know what is happening in our lives personally and professionally. During one of our telephone conversations, Beran told me he needed a general manager to run his day-to-day operations. I mentioned to him I had a friend that could be a good fit. He asked me to have this person contact him. The strength of both relationships opened a door to a position that was not advertised anywhere. They connected, but my friend ended up taking another position. Beran really appreciated the fact that I sent someone his way, even though things did not work out. These are the types of things that happen when you are involved in SuperNetworking.

Don't wait for someone to do you a favor before you do something for them. You can come up with creative ways to show reciprocity and appreciation for the people in your network. You should always be thinking about what you can do for other people. It sends a message that you care, and people will be more apt to help you when you need a favor.

I have a neighbor whose son really wanted to go to a well-known Mid-Atlantic college. He was pretty sure he had the grades to get in. I mentioned to my neighbor that I had a connection at this school and if he wished I would access my contact to see if I could help. A few months later my neighbor called and asked if I was serious about my offer to help. He did not want to impose, but it was important because it was his son's first choice. I was able to make some connections for him and his son eventually got accepted. Needless to say, the family was very appreciative. To this day, we never talk about it and I have never asked for a favor in return. However, I know if and when that day occurs, my neighbor, his wife, and his son would do anything they could to help me. They will always remember what I did for them. That's the power of what a strong network could do for you. Sometimes it's making someone's dream a reality.

Your Treasure Chest: Nourish, Develop, and Preserve It

I tell people all the time my network of contacts is my treasure chest. Heidi, a sales executive, told me her network of contacts is worth megabucks. Why? Because she invests in it every day. I found out we had a lot in common. We both pride ourselves on having access to people and information and we work on maintaining and expanding our network every day to expand our respective businesses. It sounds so simple, yet it speaks volumes. Heidi exceeds her quota every year and rarely if ever makes a cold call. She says she owes it all to the names she has in her Rolodex which she has developed and nurtured over the years.

You must treat your network of contacts as any other thing you value. It is your life-blood for future opportunities. Keep the list fresh and expand upon it. When you meet or speak to new people, immediately add their names to your database.

The reason people call me and ask for favors is because they perceive me as a person that is "well connected." They think I know everybody and stay in touch with everyone regularly. Of course I don't in fact know *everyone,* but if my ability to network makes them perceive me this way, it only serves to help me in the long term.

There are many ways to maintain the relationships or show your appreciation to your contacts and referrals. Here are a few recommendations:

▹ Add a field to your database with columns for weekly, monthly, quarterly, bi-annual, and annual. Next, look at your list of contacts and put a check in the column that makes most sense as to how often you should be speaking with them. You can cross-reference this information with the date of last contact field. This will help you track your communication, ensuring you are following up as planned.

▷ E-mail. Keep them short and sweet.

▷ Once you have landed your job, send everyone on your list a thank-you e-mail. Obviously some people were more helpful than others, but anyone whom you spoke with during the process must be thanked equally. Let them know where you will be working and provide them with your new contact information. Most importantly, be sure to offer your help to them.

▷ For the select number of people who went above and beyond when supporting you, send them a small gift to show your appreciation. This gift could be a book, golf balls, a picture, or an ornament. While it's a small gesture, make sure you put some real thought into it. These people were critical to your success and they must be recognized effectively.

▷ Send an article. If you know that the people have an interest in a certain subject, and you see an interesting article on that topic, send it along. It shows you are thinking of them.

▷ Personal updates. Let people know what's happening in your personal life—graduations, weddings, etc. This humanizes you and lets people see you in a different light.

▷ Recreational activities. Invite your contacts or referrals to go fishing, play tennis, go to a ball game, or have dinner. It's another way to keep things fresh and updated.

▷ Send holiday cards. In addition to the traditional holidays, you can stand out from the crowd by sending a card on the occasion of another holiday—include a warm note, a thank you, or a personal update.

Networking is just like what Vince Lombardi, the legendary coach of the NFL's Green Bay Packers, said about winning, "It's not a sometimes thing, it's an all-the-time thing." That's the mindset you need to have in order to be successful in finding your new job and in life.

Invest in your network of contacts, nurture those relationships, develop additional referrals, and preserve what you have every day—you will see immediate and long-term results.

Your Future's So Bright...

You need to take a long look forward to understand that the SuperNetwork you build to find a job is the beginning of a lifetime process of SuperNetworking. In the future, it will be our networks that will provide the continuity and security that long-term employment provided to earlier generations. You will know ahead of time where and when the opportunities are, and have many more options than people who do not have a SuperNetwork.

Maintaining your SuperNetwork will be your golden parachute, providing you with security for the future. You will always be able to move to the job you want, when you want. You will never have to worry about from where your next job is coming.

By learning how to develop and maintain a lifetime business network, you will always be able to reach the person you need to reach, whether they are offering a new product or service, recruiting for a job opportunity, or simply because you want to meet someone you feel you need to know.

SuperNetworking provides the dynamic infrastructure for a productive and prosperous life.

All the time you hear people saying you must network, blah, blah, blah. Few people who are actively looking for a new job have a plan like yours. You have been given a powerful, complete system that insures success.

Please help me share your networking successes with others. You might want me to be part of your network, and I might want to include you in mine. Reach out to me at *msalmon@salmonsays.com*.

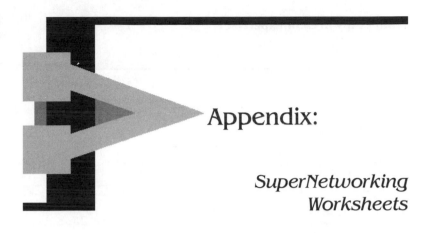

Appendix:

SuperNetworking Worksheets

STEP 1: SELF-ANALYSIS

Part I

What am I good at?

_____

_____

_____

_____

_____

_____

What is my area of expertise?

_____

_____

_____

_____

_____

What and where is my passion?

_____

_____

_____

_____

_____

_____

_____

What will make me happy?

_____

_____

_____

_____

_____

_____

What is my value to an organization?

_____

_____

_____

_____

_____

_____

_____

Where is my value to an organization?

_____

_____

_____

_____

_____

_____

_____

What should people know about me professionally?

_____

_____

_____

_____

_____

_____

_____

What should people know about me personally?

_____

_____

_____

_____

_____

_____

How have I "wowed" companies in the past?

_____

_____

_____

_____

_____

_____

_____

What would my manager say about me?

_____

_____

_____

_____

_____

_____

For what am I looking for in my next opportunity?

_____

_____

_____

_____

_____

_____

_____

Part II

Now that you have a good idea about your field of knowledge and your transferable skills, you must answer some additional questions about the type of company you want to work for.

What's the size of the company in revenue and people?

_____

_____

_____

_____

Do I want to be with a publicly-held or a privately-held company?

_____

_____

_____

Do I want to work in a start-up situation, early-stage company, or an established company?

_____

_____

_____

What type of business (high-tech, financial services, manufacturing, advertising)?

_____

_____

_____

What's the culture (formal, informal, virtual/work at home)?

_____

_____

What's the environment?

_____

_____

Geographically, how far will I commute everyday?

_____

Where is the company located? Do I want to be in the city or suburbs?

_____

What percentage of time am I willing to travel?

_____

ARTICULATION—ELEVATOR PITCH

Record the main points you want to use in your pitch and create a script.

_____

_____

_____

_____

_____

_____

_____

_____

_____

_____

_____

_____

RESEARCH PREPARATION QUESTIONS

Choose a specific person and company that you are going to call.

What does this company do and or in what industry is it?

_____

_____

_____

Based on all the research I have, it appears this company (or individual, or both) possibly needs help in which area(s)?

_____

_____

_____

_____

_____

_____

_____

Based on what I know about the company and this individual and my area of expertise, what is my value to this company or industry?

_____

_____

_____

_____

_____

_____

_____

In what area or by whom at this company (or industry) would my value to the organization (or industry) be realized?

_____

_____

_____

_____

_____

_____

What do I really "bring to the party" that is quantifiable, measurable, and makes me stand out from the crowd (both personally and professionally)?

_____

_____

_____

_____

_____

_____

_____

_____

_____

_____

_____

_____

CALL STRATEGY

Current

_____

_____

_____

_____

Alternatives

_____

_____

_____

_____

Which makes the most sense?

_____

_____

_____

_____

CALL OBJECTIVE

What do I want this person to do for me?

_____

_____

_____

_____

_____

_____

What do I want to accomplish in this phone call?

_____

_____

_____

_____

_____

_____

PHONE CALL SCRIPT

1. Setting the stage (getting their attention).

_____

_____

_____

_____

_____

_____

_____

2. Make sure you have their undivided attention.

_____

_____

_____

_____

_____

_____

_____

3. Letting them know what you are looking for (help them start to visualize and think about people they know).

_____

_____

_____

_____

_____

_____

4. Now it's time to put their feet to the fire—and also flatter them a little.

_____

_____

_____

_____

_____

_____

5. Leaving a message (They are not in, but you do want them call back ASAP).

_____

_____

_____

_____

_____

_____

_____

_____

_____

_____

_____

_____

_____

CONTACT FORM

Contact	Phone #	E-mail	Referral(s)	Company	Title, if known

Referral's Phone & E-mail	Comments	Action to be taken	Date of Contact

CONTACT FORM (CONTINUED)

Contact List

"A" List	"B" List	"C" List	"D" List

MENTOR SELECTION TOOL

Mentor Candidates (name)									
Positive Qualities	Trustworhty								
	Candor								
	Accepting								
	Available								
	Pushes you								
	Gives praise & criticism								
	Objective								
	High standards								
	Enthusiastic								
Negative Qualities	Current boss								
	Role model								
	In similar position								
	Expects money								
	Too close to me								

ACCOUNTABILITY AND RESPONSIBILIEY—WEEKLY PROGRESS FORECAST	Number of Calls Per Week	Number of New Contacts Established	Number of Resumes Sent	Number of In-person Interviews	Number of Interviews Set Up	Number of Offers Received
UNACCEPTABLE						
ACCEPTABLE						
EXCEPTIONAL						

ACCOUNTABILITY AND RESPONSIBILIEY—WEEKLY PROGRESS REPORT						
	Number of Calls Per Week	Number of New Contacts Established	Number of Resumes Sent	Number of In-person Interviews	Number of Interviews Set Up	Number of Offers Received
WEEK 1						
WEEK 2						
WEEK 3						
WEEK 4						
WEEK 5						
WEEK 6						
WEEK 7						
WEEK 8						

NEEDS, WANTS, WISHES WORKSHEET

Needs	Wants	Wishes

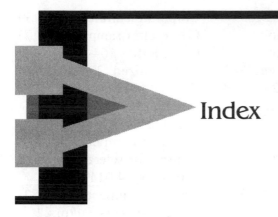

Index

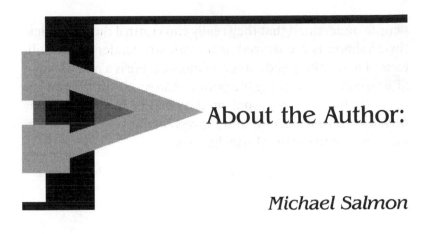

About the Author:

Michael Salmon

Michael Salmon is the founder and CEO of M. Salmon & Associates, one of the nation's leading networking training and consulting firms. Salmon delivers seminars and workshops for clients as diverse as Viacom, Fidelity Capital, New York Life, United Technologies, AT&T, Boston College Alumni Association, and St. John's University Men's Basketball team, all of which make his *SuperNetworking* ideas a powerful part of their individuals' and organizations' futures.

Salmon developed his *SuperNetworking* methodology over the course of his two decades of leadership in improving sales, marketing, and management process for both publicly traded and privately held companies. Founder of a highly successful executive search firm, which was sold to a national staffing organization, he changed the courses of many lives.

Throughout his career, he has focused on helping people discover the work they most want to do, and on helping people understand that they really can control their own destiny. Salmon is recognized as an industry leader onthe subjects of networking and career counseling. He is a much sought after speaker, explaining the power of *SuperNetworking* an has been featured in national media, including *USA Today, Investor's Business Daily,* and *Entrepreneur* magazine. He resides in Framingham, Massachusetts.